Waves

Jenna Sisick

Contents

Chapter 1

One | Little Bird

I VEY

THE HOUSE WAS EXACTLY HOW they left it.

The ancient tunnel of trees bordering the driveway shielded the harsh August sun from entering my car, but the leaves diverged at the roundabout and sent sunlight streaming through my windows. My hand flung up and blocked the rays from blinding me.

The outside had been kissed by time and a few decent storms.

Vines clung to the walls like a scared child. The white paneling was coated in a dull beige of dirt. The grass was overgrown, and the windows were smeared with water stains. The carmine red door had faded a long time ago to a pale scarlet. Even though the house had only been uninhabited for two years, the wildlife quickly reclaimed the land in tangles of green and brown. No one had been there to stop it.

"Hi, again," I whispered to the house, unable to get out of my seat. It stared back with beady eyes, almost cursing me for letting it deteriorate. It's not my fault, I wanted to say aloud like it was listening.

As if they were still here.

As if the front door would swing open from the sound of my car approaching, I would see my mom and dad standing in the doorway with open arms, tanned from the summer sun and exploration.

You promised you wouldn't cry, Ivey. So, do not start today. Somehow, I managed to avoid this place for two years. But today was the first time I was back since the accident, and every emotion I had buried for the last two years crept up like bile in my throat. Slow and steady.

It was hilarious how fictional my life had become.

The last thing I liked to do was talk about it because when I told people my parents were dead, I felt pity radiating from them like humidity before a summer storm. The conversation would grow weird, and I was suddenly treated like a house made of sticks; one wrong move, and I would fall over. Followed by a pang of guilt for ruining the mood.

So, I found it was easier to pretend they were still here, nestled inside the house on Clifton Bay, sitting in their respective dock chairs drinking coffee during sunrise. And I couldn't get ahold of them because of the slow internet. They didn't call to sing Happy Birthday because they were out on an exploration for their next research journal. We did not spend the holidays together because flights were overpriced.

It was easier to pretend than face reality.

The truth was I lived across the country. I moved from state to state doing what they raised me to do—spread my wings and study nature. It helped me forget my parents were buried five feet under the ground. Yet, standing on the brick stairs, staring into the windows, felt hollow as if someone took a butcher knife and sliced me down the middle, letting my insides pour out onto the front stoop.

I buried the thoughts, left my bags in the car, and took the small path around the house.

The tall grass swayed with the breeze from the water and tossed my hair awry. If I was staying, I would need to cut the lawn. I wondered if dad's mower was still in the shed.

The dock came into view, and I smiled for the first time since arriving. I kicked off my shoes and left them hidden in the overgrown yard. The second my feet hit the weathered wooden planks, I closed my eyes and exhaled, then began counting.

One, two, three, four... I whispered until my body wobbled at forty-six (and a half), and I opened my eyes to find my toes barely hung over the edge of the dock. My lips tugged upward into a scant smile. I still had it, I thought.

"The only thing holding you back is your mind. Remember that." I recalled my dad standing behind me, his hands on my shoulders as we stood at the beginning of the dock. I was a little over seven years old. "Close your eyes."

"What if I fall in the water?"

"Then you'll get wet." He squeezed my shoulders. "I won't let you, little bird, but I won't always be here to stop you from falling."

"Where will you be?"

His soft chuckles filled the air. "One day, you'll fly away from your mom and me. You'll have to remember what I'm teaching you now. How many steps did we count from here to the dock?"

"Forty-six and a half," I said proudly.

"And do you remember the first time we walked with our eyes closed and fell in?"

"Yes."

"That's because we didn't have a plan. But now we do. We know how many steps it takes to get to the end of the dock without falling in. I want you to remember this when you get anxious. If you fail the first time, you'll still be able to climb out of the water and learn from your mistake. Then, you make a plan, so you don't fall again. Don't stop counting, Ivey."

I never stopped counting.

Every time I joined my parents on the dock, I closed my eyes and counted until my dad proudly swept me into his arms. My eyes were still shut, and I laughed, and it bounced off the waves and dissipated into thin air. And to this day, I count when I am anxious, giving myself enough time to calm down and devise a plan.

The memories were never painful until now. Partly because when I came home in the past, I knew they would be here to create new memories, and now that I was back and nobody was here.

It was desolate.

Though, there were never many boats passing through in the first place. The occasional crabbers came to collect their traps, or fisherman visited for a bite. Yet, the only human life came from the occupants housed across and beside me.

On this side of the inlet, the water formed a Y shape. Our property veered to the right of the Y, and the tail led to the main drag of Clifton Bay. The other houses bordering the water sat further back inland, hidden by the trees. The only thing visible was their dock and occasional house lights at night.

Even then, there was minimal activity.

My eyes wandered toward the blue house across the water that mirrored ours. Everything was well kept. The regale blue paneling was still vibrant, and the back deck looked like it was freshly repainted white. I wondered who lived there now because the old occupant, Mr. Morris, was pushing eighty-one almost nine years ago, and I would be incredibly impressed if he was still alive.

No boat was tied to the moorings, and no sign of human life aside from one lone chair sat on the pristine pier. Maybe it was for sale?

Deciding it was finally time to face reality and go inside, I unpacked my car and set all of my bags in the foyer when my phone rang. My best friend Kate's name appeared on the screen, and I answered after the second ring. "Hey, you make it there safe?"

"All in one piece, sadly."

"I miss you already."

"I miss you too," I said.

"How are you holding up?"

I exhaled. My lips smacked together, making a wispy sound as I sank onto the stairs to the front door. "The tears keep trying to come out, but I just keep fighting them."

"You're allowed to cry, Ives." A moment of silence passed. "I wish you had let me come with you."

"Yeah." I rubbed the corner of my eye in slight regret. "I needed to do this on my own."

"Nobody should have to fix and sell their dead parent's house on their own. That's what I'm here for. Think about it. You could've sent me for booze and ice cream runs."

I snorted. "You think Larry would have let both of us leave?" Kate was one of the only people who talked about my dead parents like she was talking about the evening news. I loved that she did not tip-toe around me. She understood my incessant need to keep moving, and she was the only person who watched Love, Rosie with me on repeat.

"I don't care what Larry thinks. Larry can suck it."

"Don't let him hear that, or he may take you up on the offer."

She made a gagging noise, then told me she had to get back to work and to call her every day. The conversation left me feeling lighter.

My feet still hadn't budged from the ornate carpet in the foyer. I stared into the living room at the bookshelves lining the walls filled with Pierce's research journals. One's I would most likely never live up to. The worn couches and table decor were thick with a blanket of dust, keeping the lonely items warm.

Mustering up the courage, I hiked my bags onto my shoulder and made my way up the staircase to my old bedroom down the hall. I pushed the door open, flicked the light switch, and watched my green room come to life. A shiver ran through me.

My bed was made.

My curtains were drawn, revealing the perfect view of the blue house.

But nothing felt the same. I never knew it was possible to feel like a stranger in your own home.

I shut off the lights and closed the door.

DESPITE MY ROOM BEING directly above my head, I unpacked my belongings into the spare first-floor bedroom just as the sun had set beyond the waves. The red sky turned a deep royal blue, speckled with stars bright enough to see from the lack of light pollution.

My headphones filled the house's silence, and so did the hum of cicadas through the open french doors.

Albeit I was tired from days of traveling, I did not want to sleep. With my half-day-old cup of coffee, I reheated in the microwave—considering the cabinets and refrigerator were bare—I sat on the couch on the screened-in porch. The ceiling fan rattled and swirled above me, and I opened my laptop to my most recent research project.

After living in Washington State with Kate for the past four months, we were co-writing a research journal on wildlife and plants in the Pacific Northwest. She focused mainly on the animals and how they interacted, while I focused on the native plants. We were making our way down the West Coast and eventually moving to the East, where I was now.

Our boss Larry (yes, his name was Larry) made a deal that I could leave Washington early so long as our journal would be finished on time. As a bonus, I promised to write an article for the company magazine, even though that was not my job.

Sweet, old, Larry.

We had a love-hate relationship. Though it may have been one-sided.

Larry liked me a little too much, which was why he didn't want me leaving for Maryland. However, after two years of paying property tax on this abandoned house, I knew something had to change.

Wiping a trickle of sweat off my forehead, my eyes darted to the lone porch light that flickered across the bay.

A dark, burly figure emerged from the blue house, followed by a barking dog. My back straightened, and I shut my laptop, which was my sole light source. That was not Mr. Morris.

The man whistled, and the rambunctious dog returned to his side. They leisurely walked down the opposing dock together and sat in a single chair.

I did not know how long I stared and waited for my eyes to adjust. They never did.

He brought what looked to be a mug to his mouth and then, with one hand, saluted me.

Oh shit, he could see me?

I lifted my hand and waved back at the stranger across the bay.

Chapter 2

Two | Estranged Daughter

WHEN I WAS ELEVEN, my parents left me home alone for the first time.

The anxiety of them leaving hit first. It was heavy. They held me while I cried and almost did not go on their research trip. But then the exhilaration of having control hit—back when wanting responsibility was appealing, unlike now.

Even though my parents left dinner in the fridge, I remember digging in the pantry for treats. I ate all the Milano cookies on the dock while flipping through my book about trees. Mr. Morris waved to me as he fed the birds, and I waved back.

"Where are your parents, young lady?" He would ask.

"In the house," I would lie. He tried pressing further, but I never budged. I was sure Mr. Morris knew they were gone, even though it was never more than two days.

That night, after the sun went down and I was settled in bed, I locked myself in my room. The house creaked more than usual, and the pipes in the walls groaned from the summer heat. My eyes closed a total of two times, and I slept with my bedroom lights on, convinced our house was haunted.

As I got older, my parents waited until I was in high school to leave for long periods. That was when my anxiety was at its lowest, my thrill-seeking was at its highest, and I was very good at sneaking out or sneaking people in. Ghosts were not in the forefront of my mind.

But last night, I was eleven again, laying in bed with my eyes wide open.

I could have sworn I heard my parents muffled laughter above me and the sound of the coffee brewing this morning. Though, I think it was grief filling the leftover holes of their death in my heart.

So, I got up early. Instead of starting with a grocery run or my one-hundred paged house-to-do-list, I went outside at dawn and plucked different plants from the yard. The grass was wet with dew, and my feet were sopping wet. The muggy air cocooned my body, and I could barely see over the water horizon.

The man from the dock was gone, and no life graced the blue house today.

Maybe he was the younger ghost of Mr. Morris? Though, the coffee mug and dog bowl left at the edge of the dock told me the burly man was, in fact, real.

After setting my basket of new discoveries in the kitchen, I grabbed my purse and drove into town.

I followed the bends of the road, my mind subconsciously knowing where to go even though I had not lived here for nine years. I would have biked into town, but a load of groceries would not have fit in the tiny basket.

The paved road turned to rocky red brick as the old-fashioned town came into view.

Boats rocked in the harbor beneath the hidden sun, and the sleepy town slowly stirred awake. People walked with their dogs or partner, and others sat with a cup of coffee outside of Oliver's Cafe. I watched small store owners flip their closed signs to open and shifted in my seat.

My head buzzed with discomfort. I felt the stares before I saw them. Did people know it was me, or was it the lack of recognition that made them look? With faint smiles in their direction, I beelined into the grocery store and shopped faster than ever before.

"Did you see someone is staying at the Pierce house?"

"Tragic what happened to that family."

"Do they have any kids?"

"Just an estranged daughter."

"Estranged?"

"I think that's her."

And so it started. My stomach turned upside down from the conversation, but I didn't turn to look and set all of my groceries on the checkout counter. The older woman smiled at me; her eyes lingered on my face between each item scan. "Having a good start to the morning, Hun?"

"Yeah, thanks. And you?"

She nodded. "You're a pretty thing," she said. "And look awfully familiar too."

It was not that I didn't want people to know who I was or that I was back in town, but it was the pity I would receive once people realized I had returned. Everyone grieved when my parents died, but I never came back to let people grieve with me or share their condolences, and their sympathy was left unheard.

Before I had the chance to speak, she squinted and leaned forward. "I know you... You're the Pierce girl."

I chuckled nervously. "Ivey, yeah."

"My God, you're a grown-up! Have you been back long?"

"I got back last night."

Her lips pressed together in a sad smile as she swiped my credit card. She paused before she asked, "How have you been?"

"I've been okay." I smiled and loaded my groceries into the cart, neglecting to show any signs of sadness. "This is a random question, but do you know if Mr. Morris, Peter Morris," I corrected. "Still lives on Clifton Bay?"

Her face fell. "Mr. Morris passed away a year ago, Hun."

"Oh." So someone new lived there.

Our conversation turned relatively light for the next few minutes. I avoided any more talk of my parents, then meandered to my car and drove back to my house. I was relieved to be back, hidden in the privacy of my home.

THE NEXT COUPLE OF DAYS were like groundhogs day. I woke, threw on the shittiest clothes I owned, and worked outside until sunset. The yard needed more attention than the interior, and if I wanted to sell the house without breaking my bank account, I figured I would do everything on my own.

It couldn't be that bad, could it? It was already therapeutic, despite my aching muscles, and the showers were the best reward.

Since my grocery store trip, I avoided venturing into town like the plague, and my dinners mainly consisted of take-out. I had more leftover pizza than I could consume, but I went to bed each night with a full belly and woke up to eat another cold slice.

After showering, I took my mug and laptop and walked to the edge of the dock to watch the sunset, but when I got to the bottom, I turned around. "The chairs," I said and set my stuff down on the wood.

When I dug the lawn mower out of the shed earlier in the week, I found my parent's dock chairs hidden inside. I wasn't sure why they were tucked away and not on the dock, but at least they were still intact.

With all my might, I lifted my mom's Adirondack chair and carried it down the dock.

Halfway there, I lurched forward, and the chair I carried clattered onto its side. My body hit the wood, and pain seared through my foot and up my leg in shock waves. "Damnit! Shit!" I cradled my bloody foot, cussing more.

I scanned the area until I saw the culprit—a bloody nail sticking from the planks.

"You alright?" A deep voice bellowed over the water, followed by the distant clanking of heavy footsteps.

My head darted upward from behind the fallen chair, and I caught a glimpse of my neighbor standing at the foot of his dock. There were roughly sixty feet of water between us, and it was rather dark, but I saw his chest heaving from running. That was definitely not Mr. Morris's ghost.

"I'm fine. I just stepped on a fucking nail."

He forked his fingers through his hair. "Is the nail still in your foot?"

"No."

"Are you bleeding?"

"A lot," I laughed in stress while staring at the sticky mess.

"Hang tight," he said and jogged toward his house. Was he coming here? I heard a door slam, faint muffled barking, and then the roar of an engine. Behind the darkness of trees bordering the right side of Mr. Morris's property, a small motorboat coasted into the bay.

The ground shuttered beneath me as his boast glided against my dock.

The neighbor hopped out, slugged the rope around the metal mooring, and strode toward me. He sat my mother's chair upright and bent down onto one knee. "Wow," he blew through pursed lips. "That is a lot of blood."

"I told you," I said, trying not to stare, but I was doing terribly.

This man was the definition of handsome. He towered over me (maybe because he was standing), and his wrinkled black tee-shirt was snug on his arms. I could not help but notice the five-o'clock shadow decorating his chin.

Like me, he looked—and smelled—fresh out of the shower. Yet his damp, light brown hair sat perfectly on his head while the heat twisted mine into frizzy waves. Not to mention, I did not have a bra on, and this tank-top was doing nothing to hide my breast.

"Let's get you in this chair."

He set his first aid kit down and held out his broad hands. My stomach swelled, but instead of taking his help—since I was covered in blood—I pushed myself off the ground and wobbled. At the speed of light, he gripped my hips and stabilized me.

Our eyes locked, and his narrowed. They were dark, dense, like an unpenetrable boulder I could not see through.

He didn't say anything more as he guided me the rest of the way into the seat and crouched to look at my foot. "I can barely see out here." He used his phone flashlight to look at my wound. The tiny solar-paneled lights bordering the dock did not give much light. "I'll help you into the house."

"The house?"

He paused and looked at me as though I spoke another language. "Yeah, your house. The one behind you."

I blinked. "I've never seen you before."

"I've never seen you either."

It fell silent.

"Do you want my help or not?" he asked.

I stared at the brown-eyed man, then nodded, realizing I would have to limp back without my things. Who cares if he saw your mess, Ivey. So, I held my hand out, and we hobbled toward the back door.

"The kitchen is this way." I pointed into the dark, evergreen-colored room and flicked on the light switch, terribly aware of his grip on me.

The space lit up, and his eyes immediately darted toward the mess of leaves and plants on the island. I would've used my parent's old office for my recreational research, but I hadn't mustered the courage to go inside yet.

"Sorry about the mess." I brushed the dirt off the counter, though it fell into a tiny pile on the wood floor. I puckered my lips to blow when he wasn't looking but resided up kicking it away with my unscathed foot.

"Why are you apologizing?"

"I-I don't know." I saw him much clearer now, but all I noticed was apathy. "Because there is dirt on my kitchen counter."

He shrugged like he didn't care and knelt. Unzipping the first aid kit he brought, he asked if I had any hydrogen peroxide, and I pointed towards the sink. I watched him mix it with water, dunk a gauze pad into the solution, and hold it to my arch. My jaw clenched.

The stranger didn't speak. He moved easily, cleaning the blood and wrapping my foot with a long piece of gauze. Back and forth, back and forth, his hands glided. If I had to guess, he had done this before.

Strange didn't begin to cover how I felt. "What's your name?"

"Weston."

I waited for him to ask mine, but he never did.

"Thanks for helping me, Weston."

"Yep."

Okay, then.

For the next five minutes, he secured the dressing and gathered all the wrappers. Wordlessly, I pointed to the bin, and he tossed the trash inside and peeled the rubber gloves off. Without taking my eyes off him, I stood to follow him out, despite my ailment.

"You don't have to show me out."

"I'm not showing you out. I have to get the stuff I left outside." I neglected his advice and slipped on sandals so I didn't ruin his handy-work in the wet grass and followed him out the door. He walked at a much faster pace, and it took a lot of balance to keep up. I could have sworn he was running.

But then, he stopped and my pace slowed. He bent down and picked up my mom's chair laying beside my puddle of blood and carried it to the end of the dock where it used to reside.

A tender throbbing ebbed through my chest from the gesture, and the sight of my parent's chair in its rightful spot had me gnawing on the inside of my cheek in an attempt to chew away the unwanted emotions. He did not have to do that.

I made it to his boat a couple of seconds after. Slightly out of breath, I snorted at the rope. They hung loose, and the vessel wobbled with the high tide, slamming against the wood in lilting jerks. "Your boats gonna float away if you tie it like that."

"What?" He glanced between me and where it was poorly secured to the post.

"That's not how you tie a boat."

He stared deadpan. I did everything not to fidget, but he made me want to crawl out of my skin. I had never met anyone with such a lack of emotion. Except there had to be something behind those dull eyes to help a random woman with their bloody foot.

"Come by the old doctor's office tomorrow on Oyster street." A thud rang when his feet hit the metal floor of his boat. "You will need a tetanus shot."

"What time—"

"Just stop by whenever. I'll get you in."

What did he mean he'd get me in? Did he work there? What happened to Dr. Wagner?

Before I could ask any more questions, he zipped toward the shadow of trees and vanished behind them. Silence fell over the water, a single wallop of a door closing echoed, and the porch lights to the house flickered off.

□□□□□□□□✹□□□□□□□□

QOTD: What's your favorite opening line from a novel?

□□□□□□□□✹□□□□□□□□

Chapter 3

Three | Blue House Ghost

I WAITED UNTIL THE LAST possible moment to drive into town.

It took a lot of contemplation, but the last thing I wanted was for my body to freeze and die from tetanus, simply because I did not want to deal with the blue house ghost again—who was called Weston now.

The town's main drag was linked by connecting walls and narrow alleyways where local restaurants, a lone floral shop (run by the same family) a library, and Oliver's Coffee shop stood. An old church sat haphazardly on its foundation at the end of the street. The view of the sparkling water behind it.

Amidst everything was a beige-bricked building older than every resident here.

The creaking of a rusty metal sign screeched above the door. It still had Dr. Wagner's name etched into the wood, but on the front door was a makeshift sign that read—

Weston Turner, Advanced Practice Registered Nurse

Nurse Practitioner. Now it made sense; it was his duty to help me, not a desire. No wonder he was so apathetic last night. Some random woman cuts her foot on a nail, and he feels morally obligated to help.

I pushed through the front door. The stale scent of wicker chairs and expired mint filled my nose, sending me back in my memories to when my parents brought me here when I was younger. I left with a cherry lollipop each time.

The secretary who had been here as long as Dr. Wagner greeted me by pushing her glasses further up the bridge of her nose. "Hi, what can I do for you?"

"Hi, I'm here to see Weston Turner."

"Do you have an appointment?"

"I don't." I paused, rocking on my heels. "Could you tell him Ivey Pierce is here?" The moment the question left my mouth, I internally swore at myself. Weston did not know my name because I never told him. Because he didn't care enough to ask.

Her harsh features softened. "Are you Logan and Ester's daughter?"

Here we go. "I am."

"It's wonderful to see you again, Ivey. I'm so sorry for your loss."

Even though I hadn't known this woman personally, I told her it was great to see her again too and thanked her because that's what my parents would have wanted.

Just as I was about to explain how Weston didn't know my name, the door to the right of the front desk opened.

Our eyes locked first, and he looked different in this light.

He wore black slacks, a light blue button-up shirt with a patternless navy tie. A white lab coat donned his shoulders, and a stethoscope hung loosely around his neck. It had been a while since I had seen a man so well kept. Most of the men I worked with wore hiking boots and crouched behind trees—that's if we weren't in the office.

"Ivey?" My name rolled off his lips with uncertainty.

"That's me." I patted the counter, showing a faint smile. He stepped aside so I could follow. He was silent like most of last evening, and walking behind him felt like I was getting sucked into a massive black hole—my mind went mush.

Weston must've been new to town, especially since Mr. Morris only passed a year ago for his house to be up for sale, and Dr. Wagner would not have left his practice unless it was over his dead body. So, it was safe to assume Dr. Wagner had passed too. Was everyone dying here? I made a mental note not to drink out of the tap.

We abruptly turned into a small outdated room with floral patterned wallpaper and tile floors.

He pointed to the examination table. "You can sit there."

The paper crinkled beneath me as I wiggled onto the bench. "Have you given a lot of these?"

His brows drew together. "Tetanus shots?" he clarified, pumping soap into his large hands and scrubbing. I nodded. "Yeah, I have."

"So it won't hurt?"

"It's a needle. All needles hurt to some extent."

A short laugh rolled from my lips, and he turned to look at me. My smile faltered when I saw his flat expression. Jeez. I wanted to tell him to lighten up. "I've never heard a medical professional say that."

"Do you want me to lie?"

"I mean," I swung my feet like a child. "A little lie would be nice."

"I don't see a point in lying when we both know the truth." He dried his hands and sat on the swivel stool. "Needles don't feel nice. I don't like getting poked, and neither do my patients, no matter how much I butter them up. I have found it's easier to tell them it hurts, so they're expecting the worse, and when they get the real deal, it is not nearly as bad as their mind made it out to be."

I stifled a smile. That was the most words he had spoken since we met. "Makes sense."

"So no, Ivey, it won't feel nice but I'll be quick."

My stomach rippled when he said my name and wheeled closer. His knees almost brushed mine, and his head was in line with my upper ribcage, but from how low he was to the ground, it looked like he was staring up at my breasts.

I didn't say anything else, and he stood and pulled over a tray with the booster equipment. "Which arm do you prefer?"

"Uh, my right."

"Are you right-handed?"

"Yes."

"Then you should probably do your left. Your arm may be sore after."

Then why did you ask which arm I preferred?

"Alright." I unbuttoned the top of my long-sleeve, light cotton shirt and slipped the fabric off my shoulder as he put gloves on. When he turned around, he looked at my bare skin, face, then back to my arm.

He placed his two fingers on my shoulder. "Relax your arm."

"I am."

"I can feel you tensing."

I closed my eyes, breathed, and let my whole body sag. The scent of rubbing alcohol filled the air, and my skin felt cold as he cleansed and counted before pushing the needle into my muscle. My forehead wrinkled in discomfort, yet before I knew it, he stuck a bandaid to my arm and cleaned up.

This man was stranger than I thought. I couldn't tell if his hard outer shell was a result of being burned by people, or if that was simply his personality. Either way, it should've turned me away but I wanted to pry.

"Can I look at your foot while you're here?" he asked.

"You'll have to pay to see my foot."

He paused. "I'll bill your insurance."

Was that a joke? Laughter bubbled out of me, and I could not help but watch to see if a smile budged on his face, except he had turned his back before I got the chance. It seemed Mr. I-never-smile does have some sense of humor buried in that empty vessel.

I scooted further back on the table, so my leg rested straight. Weston sat down on the stool and unwrapped his bandage work. "Maybe instead of billing your insurance, I'll give you money for a pedicure."

My jaw practically hit the floor. "Are you saying my feet are ugly?" My polish was chipped, and working in the yard gave me callouses, not soft feet. He glanced at me through his lashes but didn't answer my question.

"So, what do I call you? Doctor?"

"I'm not a doctor, so no. Usually, people call me Mr. Turner or just Weston."

"Mr. Turner," I said aloud to see how it sounded. "Have you been in town long?"

"Six months."

I wanted to ask more questions but didn't. I sounded like a true Clifton local, grilling people on information they were not obligated to share. If I had learned anything about Weston, he was reserved and maybe a tiny asshole. Not a complete ass, more-so vain. Yet, I could have entirely misjudged him. Clifton did bring out the viciousness in people.

He worked with his head down. I stared at his thick head of hair, occasionally catching glimpse of the bridge of his nose and long lashes. When the new bandages were in place, he removed his gloves and rewashed his hands.

When he didn't say anything else, I asked, "Is that it then?"

"Yeah, you can meet the secretary Lisa at the front desk, and she'll get you situated."

I thanked him for his helped and received a nod in return, then showed myself to the front. The secretary smiled when I approached the front desk, and Weston followed suit, handing her a piece of paper from behind the glass.

Two ladies in the waiting room whispered while Lisa asked for my insurance card.

"Did you hear he slept with Nora's daughter before she went back to New York? Real professional."

"Yeah, I did. I would've gone to a different office if this wasn't the only one in town. Talk about professionalism."

Lisa peered over my shoulder, and her glasses slid down her nose as she looked over the top lens. Her hands still moved, swiping my card and typing out of muscle memory as we both eavesdropped on the not-so-quiet conversation I suspected was about Weston.

I was no better than them because I was trying to listen.

The secretary and I shared a knowing look. She shook her head ever-so-slightly, and it made me smile. "You're all set to go, Ivey."

The tiny bell above the front door jingled when I pushed it open, announcing my departure. Yet, I couldn't help but look back into the office when Weston called out for his next patient—one of the gossiping women. She stood, glowered at her friend, then smiled fictitiously at the nurse practitioner.

I was the last thing he looked at before his shoulders slumped, and he pulled the door closed.

□□□□□□□□❀□□□□□□□□

QOTD: What is your favorite plant/flower?

Hi friends :) I don't quite have an update schedule for BTW yet, once I do, I'll let you all know! Are you liking it so far?

vote • comment • follow

Thanks for reading ♡

□□□□□□□□❀□□□□□□□□

Chapter 4

Four | Gossiping, Nosey Cog

"YOU STEPPED ON A NAIL? Are you alright?" Kate's voice rang into the backyard as my knees made indents in the dirt and my fingers yanked weeds out of the ground. I turned down my phone speaker, dragging my arm across my forehead.

My tanning lotion slipped off my skin like oil on a hot surface while the sun continued baking me alive. "Yeah, and get this," my voice hushed because I knew how easily sound carried over water. "This new mysterious neighbor guy came to my rescue."

"A mysterious man? Tell me more." I told her everything from him coming inside my house to me getting a tetanus shot a couple of days ago. Then her tone changed. "Ivey..."

"I already know what you're going to say."

"I was going to tell you what you told me to say if you got distract-ed."

"I'm not distracted. Talk to all the blisters I'll have on my fingers and knees from the yard work I've done today." I brushed the dirt off my palms and rested back on my heels. "You have no idea what Clifton is like. The moment you cross the county line, the town sucks you into its vortex, and you become this gossiping, nosey cog who feeds off drama and other people's business."

She snorted. "Wow, who am I talking to right now? I don't know this version of Ivey. Put my friend back on the phone."

Even though I knew she was joking, my whole body sagged at her remark, and I stared up at the house—the reason I was here. "If I lose myself, I'll call Larry and have you shipped over here."

"As always, fuck Larry. I will come now if you need me."

My lips turned up into a soft smile.

"So what's the deal with this guy?" she asked.

The urge to look at his house nipped at me, so I craned my head and was met with the lifeless property. Water lapped against his motorboat, and the trees lining his property swayed with the afternoon breeze.

Not that I was watching, but I noticed he only came out at night or very early in the morning, which I concluded was because of his job or because he was a vampire. Neither were terrible options. "I think it's because I know nothing about him except that he's been here for six months. People are usually born and die here in Clifton, and the locals don't seem to like him very much even though he is very nice to look at."

"Oh, how come? Do you know why?"

"Nope. But I did hear someone say he fucked someone's daughter without any more context. I have no idea, but everyone judges me here too because I had a private funeral for my parents and didn't let anyone attend, then left, so I know how he feels."

"So he's a ladies' man?"

"I wouldn't say that. I'm a lady, and he talks to me like he's talking to a brick wall."

"Well, I guess it's good to keep it that way. If he talked to you like you were the sexiest woman alive, which you are, you'd definitely be distracted."

I laughed at her compliment, and we continued talking about my experience so far in Clifton and her time in Washington State. We ended the call by confirming what else I had to write for our research journal. As I pulled more weeds and sprinkled mulch in their place, my brain would not shut off despite cranking my music up.

No matter how much time passed between graduating high school and now, I still felt like a child. I thought it would subside as days passed, but it only worsened. It was partly because my routine was off, and the feeling my parents would waltz through the front door any second lingered in my chest.

Though, the house and I had slowly become acquaintances again. The walls and floors had stopped groaning at night, I didn't smell coffee brewing in the early mornings, and the house welcomed me with open arms anytime I came back from town, overwhelmed by the leering eyes and hushed talk.

I always dreamt of living in a house tucked away from the hustle of life. A home where I could sleep with the windows open, listen to the cicadas sing at night, and step outside on a sticky morning with a cup of coffee while the dew hung heavily in the air. Except, now I was here and never felt so alone, which was why my mind constantly lingered on the man in the blue house.

Weston might've been across the bay, but it was comforting knowing someone was close enough if I needed help, and even if he didn't want to see me, I could get the family boat out of the boat garage and sail over.

By late afternoon, the sun had lost its swelter, and I retreated inside to wash today's grime away and eat dinner. Still, my fridge looked barren, with no leftovers or fresh produce. I could have skipped dinner or made butter noodles. Instead, I hopped on my bike, pushed through the searing pain in my foot, and rode toward town.

As I whirled past quaint lake houses and watched porch lights turn on, all was quiet aside from the whooshing wind in my ears. The sky melded into dusky shades of blues, and I closed my eyes briefly and smiled.

I hoped this grocery run would be swift, and I could slip in and out of the store without being stopped for a conversation. Despite being here for almost a week, I had ventured out twice. Once for the first grocery trip and second for the tetanus shot, meaning nobody has been able to corner me.

I chained my bike and entered the store, filling my basket with only the needed things. The isles were desolate, and the harsh buzzing of the fluorescent lights and hum from the refrigerators lining the walls was all I heard.

Yet, my heart skipped a beat when I turned into the ice cream section.

Weston stood at the freezer with a basket in hand and ice cream in the other. For some reason, he didn't seem like someone who would buy ice cream. I'd expect him to eat tubs of greek yogurt with slices of fresh fruit and a strong cup of black coffee. With all that bitterness, maybe he chews the raw coffee beans?

His brows cinched as he read the label, still in his formal attire from the office. Though the tie was gone, I couldn't help but stare at the top undone buttons of his shirt. Although he looked like he belonged in Clifton in that outfit, he radiated outsider energy.

"That is a good flavor," I said to my neighbor.

His head whirled at the sound of my voice, and his hands fell to his side. Then he reread the label as though he had forgotten the flavor he was holding. "It is."

I stepped closer and reached for the freezer, grabbing my pint of cookie dough. He didn't take his eyes off me as I stuck it in my basket and smiled faintly. I hoped he would smile back but was not lucky.

Rocking on my heels once, I thought of something to say. "I haven't seen you on your dock." That was weird. Now he will think I was looking at his house, even though I was.

"Yeah, I've been busy. Have you managed to step on any more nails?"

It took a beat to register the playfulness through his stoic expression, but when I did, I faked a laugh. "Ha Ha, very funny, but no."

"I hope you're giving that foot a rest." He motioned to the appendage, still causing a limp in my step.

"Oh, I am," I lied. "Thanks for helping me again."

"Have you fixed the dock?" He put the container of ice cream back in the freezer instead of his basket and began walking. I took the question as an invitation to follow.

He picked a couple of items from the shelves as I answered. "No, I haven't got around to it yet."

"Are you renovating or something?"

"More like straightening up the place."

"To sell?" He asked. I glanced at the few people surrounding us, including the lady at the register who rang me up on the first day. I noticed their fleeting stares as we meandered the isles. They watched us like we were stray animals, digging in their garbage, and the last thing I wanted was for them to overhear our conversation.

"I don't know yet."

He slowed and looked at me, then at the others in the store. I watched the wheels turn in his head, and when our eyes locked for a second time, I knew he understood my answer—or lack of it. There was something cathartic about his awareness.

We parted ways to finish shopping but reunited at the register, with him in line behind me.

"Hey, Hun." The cashier smiled as I placed the food on the conveyor belt. "Nice to see you again."

"You too." A full second barely passed before I caught her shrewd inspection of the light-brown-haired practitioner over my shoulder.

My forehead wrinkled, and when she faced me again, her darkened eyes widened, and her lips curled up as though she had not been judging him.

"You've been cooped up in that house for a couple of days. I'm glad to see you out in town."

I was about to tell her I had been busy, but I did not want her asking what. "It's great to get out."

"You know, we have a town meeting every Wednesday evening at Town Hall. It's super laid back, and Oliver supplies pastries and coffee. You're a resident, so you're always welcome to join. I'm sure everyone would love to see your beautiful face again."

I noticed her emphasis on 'you're a resident and a second sideways glance at Weston.

Their town meetings were code for politically correct gossip sessions. My parents used to go as a form of entertainment and report back to me with croissants and scandals. Clifton's version of a scandal was as frivolous as someone wearing white after Labor day.

There was no doubt she had an issue with Weston, just like the ladies in his office waiting room, which only made me want to push her buttons further. He may have been a little on the emotionless side, but I was not going to let their attitude slide.

"Thanks for the offer." I turned to my neighbor, stooping to their level. "Do you attend the meetings since you are the town practitioner?"

"I wasn't aware of these meetings." His hands fisted his pockets, and he leaned against the register counter.

"That's odd for someone devoting their time to caring for sick patients."

The cashier looked between us, h mouth hanging open slightly. "Nobody has invited you?" The shock in her voice was over-enthusiastic. "How strange. Feel free to join us too, Mr. Turner. The town would love to get to know you."

He nodded, and the rest of the conversation fell flat.

Triumph simmered through me. I had done my job.

I slid my grocery bags onto my arms as Weston unpacked his basket. When I thought I could leave unscathed, the woman caught my attention one last time. "I don't know if you're aware since it's been ages, but there is a memorial for your parents at Cliff beach. I'm sure they would love it if you paid a visit. A lot of people put great effort into it."

My veins went icy, and the hissing electricity sounded like it was coming from inside my head. I hardly cracked a smile as I thanked her for the information about my parent's memorial and hurried outside without looking at Weston.

The humid air did nothing to help my needy lungs.

Something about her comment struck a cord. Who was she to say my parents would love it if I visited a memorial nobody told me about? I had dealt with my grief, been to therapy for my trauma, learned to cope with the tragedy of their death, and I didn't need a monument or shrine to remember them.

Maybe the town needed a memorial because I didn't give them a chance to say goodbye at a funeral, but that didn't mean I didn't say goodbye. That did not mean I didn't mourn every day.

Hopping on my bike, my legs burned as I pedaled home.

The four walls and roof at the end of the street were the only thing keeping me going until a car zoomed past and slowed to my pace. I looked to my right as Weston rolled down the window to his black car. "You biked to town with that foot?" his voice rang over the noise from the engine.

"I needed the fresh air!"

"Cars have windows."

I slammed on my breaks. Seconds later, his tires screeched to a halt, and he put his car in reverse and backed up until we were face to face again. His chiseled features were incredibly displeased with me as he glanced at my foot.

"You're in the middle of the road."

He ignored my comment. "Get in the car, and I'll give you a ride back."

"Why?"

"Because I don't want you biking on that wound."

"My wound is fine."

"I disagree."

I laughed and shook my head, pushing forward. "I don't take rides from strangers."

He followed beside me. "I'm not a stranger. I'm your neighbor."

"Well, actually, Weston, that still makes us strangers. I know nothing about you."

"You know my name, where I work and live."

I slammed on my breaks again, and so did he. Was I really going to take him up on his offer? I would consider him somewhere between a stranger and an acquaintance, although I still expected there was an ultimatum behind the ride. Nevertheless, I climbed off my bicycle and collected my groceries out of the basket.

He put his hazard lights on and got out of his car, wheeling my bike to the trunk. I slid into the passenger seat as two cars sped past. The vehicle rocked when he slammed the driver's door and started toward my house.

His car smelled of mahogany and rain on a hot summer day. I couldn't tell if it was coming from him or the open windows, but I closed my eyes and took a deep breath. "Thanks for driving me."

His knuckles turned white as he gripped the steering wheel. "No problem."

As the paved road turned rocky, I pointed him toward my house. He pulled up to the front door, and I watched him scan the house from top to bottom, probably analyzing the dreary state of the place.

We met at the trunk as he hoisted my bike out of the car. "Thanks again for the ride."

"Sure thing." He put his hands in his pockets, and I watched his lips purse and then relax. I could tell he wanted to say something but didn't.

Like children, we stared at one another in silence, unable to say goodbye. I don't know how long we stood there before he climbed into his car and drove through the canopy of trees, past the front gate, and out of sight.

□□□□□□□□❀□□□□□□□□

QOTD: Reply to the person above you and then post your own comment for people to reply to!

vote • comment • follow

Thanks for reading ♡

□□□□□□□□❀□□□□□□□□

Chapter 5
Five | Handy Man

THUMP, THUMP, THUMP.

My eyes sprung open, and I brushed my hair out of my sleepy face. It took a second for my eyes to adjust, but when they did, I noticed there was no sunlight streaming through the cracks in my blinds. What time was it, and what was that sound? I paused, waiting to hear the noise again.

When one didn't come, my lids fluttered shut, still heavy with morning drowsiness.

Thump, thump, thump.

My body jerked upright, and I grabbed my tee shirt, which found its way off my body from a middle-of-the-night heat stroke. I meandered through the living room, stumbling over my feet, past the kitchen to the wall of windows. The sound had to be coming from outside.

Like a camera trying to focus, my eyes adjusted on the backyard—squinting then growing wide. What the hell? A figure knelt on my dock, almost hidden behind the brush of trees, beating the planks with a hammer. The sound of the metal rang out into the dawn.

I could not see the stranger's face, but from the looks of the terribly tied boat and dog lying at the end of my dock, I assumed it was Weston.

The growing pressure in my chest from the view made me grip the window frame.

Why he was helping me was beyond any answer I had. I didn't think Weston was the type to wake up at five and fix a stranger's dock, but it seems I misjudged him.

He drove you home, too, Ivey. I wondered if he noticed my shift in emotion last night when the cashier spoke about my parents. Unlike the town gossip sessions, my parents' death was the most fascinating thing to happen here, which only meant they continuously exploited it for all it was worth, no matter how gruesome and traumatic it was. I was sure Weston had heard the story by now, and if he hadn't, last night probably raised questions.

Not wanting to scare him off, I took my time waking up, getting dressed, and peeking out the windows every time I passed. He worked his way further and further down the landing. Curiosity nipped at me like claws when I sat at the kitchen island, waiting for my coffee pot to brew.

I pulled my phone out and texted Kate, knowing she'd be awake by now. Neighbor nurse hottie is on my dock.

She replied, Mysterious guy? The one you're not supposed to be distracted by?

Yes. He's distracting me.

Oh, no. What is he doing on your dock?

I glanced out the window and typed, He is fixing it.

Weston leaned back on his heels and fisted a hand through his hair. A high-pitched, faint noise resonated, barely audible through the glass. His dog jumped from the end of the dock and dashed toward Weston's open arms. The white and red-furred friend looked like a gentle giant with short fluffy hair and a droopy face. If I had to guess, it looked like a Saint Bernard, but I didn't know dog breeds well.

Weston's back faced me, but I imagined the apples of his cheeks plump and his eyes crinkled at the edges while the dog licked his face.

That was if he could smile.

Kate texted back, The nurse practitioner is also a handyman? What a know-it-all. I bet he plays the guitar too.

I laughed at my best friend's message. I'm going to talk to him. I typed, shoved my phone into my jean pocket, and opened the cupboard. My heart stalled like a car running out of gas when I saw my parent's mugs sitting front and center, with dust collecting around the base in a fuzzy sheet.

No matter how often I had seen the unused cups, it felt like a hot knife plunging deep into my belly. I could not think about them now. I reached past them, collecting a mug for Weston—rinsing any grime out—and poured us each a heaping cup.

The wet grass, slick with morning moisture, squished between my toes. "Want a coffee?" I broke the silence. His neck and the dogs snapped in my direction. The giant bolted for me, its tongue hanging out of its mouth as it circled my legs.

"Ah! Masie!" Weston stood and clapped his hands. "Come."

Masie didn't listen. She bumped my legs and looked up, her eyes gleaming with excitement. The brimming mugs wobbled in my hand, and a chuckle slipped from my lips. "I'm so sorry I can't pet you right now, Masie. My hands are full."

Weston took the hint and took the cup I extended. "Thank you."

"I don't know how you take your coffee, so it's plain."

"That's fine." He took a hearty sip. I was right, and he did like strong coffee.

I crouched to pet Masie. She took the invitation and pressed against me, drool dribbling from her mouth. "Can I ask what you're doing on my dock this bright and early?"

"Fixing the nails." He motioned to the mess behind him as though he were discussing the weather. I blinked, bewildered, while he wiped the sweat off his forehead. I wanted to ask why he was fixing my dock, but I kept our small talking going.

"Don't you work today?"

"I'm on call during the weekends."

"So if I stepped on another nail—"

"I'd have to go to work."

I snorted. "Well, good thing you're taking them all away." Corner and bombard him with questions, Ivey, my conscious coaxed me. "Do you want to sit for a minute?"

He nodded, and I walked past him down the length of the dock, avoiding stepping on any of his handy work. I noticed the ragged nails protruding through the wood were gone, replaced with new ones, flesh against the planks.

Warmth simmered through me, but I smothered it before it reached my heart.

"You can sit." I motioned to my mom's chair and plopped on the edge of the dock, submerging my feet into the cool, murky water.

Fog rested over the bay like a rug while the sun tried to shine through the thickness of dawn. It was unsuccessful; grayness hung in the atmosphere, and the water stood still like glass.

Masie sat beside me like a good girl, and I rested my arm over her back.

I swear I heard a sigh behind me. I turned to look at Weston standing beside my mother's chair. "First you bike, then walk in the mud barefoot, now you're soaking your foot in a bacteria-infested bay. You're a terrible patient."

"Just like all the Clifton housewives? Sometimes this town feels like it's straight out of Big Little Lies when I really want Stars Hollow."

His brow lifted. "I'm not licensed to amputate."

"Oh, really? I thought I heard a rumor that was what you did in the office basement." I leaned in. "For free, even."

His lip twitched like his brow, and my heart flip-flopped. Was that an almost smile?

"I'm sure you've heard a lot of rumors about me."

I scoffed. "I'm sure you've heard a lot about me too."

Neither of us asked about the rumors. Instead, we sat (well, Weston stood, I sat) in silence. I wanted to know if the whispers about Weston were true—not that I would judge him for them—yet I buried the Clifton personality clawing its way out of me.

"So, am I picking you up Wednesday for the town meeting?"

I choked on my coffee. "You know, we don't have to go, and I was just being a pain."

His eyes searched mine before he said, "I know." His observation hung thick in the air, and I wondered if it was his strange way of saying thank you for having his back yesterday. If only I was snarkier toward the cashier.

"Won't you be in town already for work?"

"I'll be back before seven. I'll pick you up."

"Okay." I fidgeted with my mug. "Well, if you raincheck, I won't be upset."

"Do you want me to raincheck?"

"I didn't say that. I'm simply giving you an out if you change your mind." I shrugged. His standing made me antsy. "You know you can sit down?"

"I should get back to work before the sun is up. Thank you for the coffee."

I pushed onto my feet, wondering what was going through his head. The fact he wanted to go to the meeting surprised me but also ignited excitement I forgot was possible to feel. My heart wanted to call it a date, but my brain settled on the "revenge outing" title.

"Thank you again for fixing the dock. If you need to use the bathroom or need water, just knock on the back door. I'll be working inside today." I took his empty mug and spotted the rope holding his boat to the mooring loosen with every lapping wave. "Oh, by the way, you need to get better at tying your boat."

I knelt beside the berth and retied the rope.

"Where'd you learn to do that?"

"I lived here for nineteen years." I brushed my hands on my jeans, picking up the mugs again. "You've got a lot to learn about me, Weston."

"I see that," he said. When I glanced in his direction, I saw the remnants of a smile caressing the corner of his lips.

□□□□□□□□ ✿ □□□□□□□□

QOTD: How do you de-stress?

vote • comment • follow

Thanks for reading ♡

□□□□□□□□ ✿ □□□□□□□□

Chapter 6

Six | The Rain

I USED TO LOVE the rain, especially the smell as it mixed with the earth.

It rolled off the porch roof in heavy beads and pooled in the yard. The house shook as the wind changed directions, slamming sideways into the shingles. It was hard enough that I felt the rattle in my chest. I made a mental note to unclog the gutters since they weren't doing their job, but I watched the monsoon fall for now.

Rain was to the earth as oxygen was to our lungs.

All of the things I studied thrived off the element. Without it, crops wouldn't flourish, animals would die, and rivers would dry up. I wouldn't have a job or anything to write about. Though, sometimes, I thought about what my life would be like if it didn't rain.

Maybe my parents would still be alive.

I looked up from my computer, dampened my skin from the mist blowing through the porch screen, and closed my eyes.

"They're not picking up, Kate."

"Let me try. What are the satellite digits again?"

I repeated my parent's satellite phone number they always took on their research projects as I paced the length of my apartment. The TV glowed through the darkness, and the news castor's voice sounded like the teacher from Charlie Brown. I could not continue listening to how destructive the East Coast storms were.

"Nothing. They are not picking up."

I pressed my palms against my sockets. "Fuck! Kate. Am I going to have to call 911?"

My best friend stared at me from the lone armchair in my living room, her shoulders stiff. "Are you positive they have their phone with them?"

"Yes, they call me every evening."

"And you talked to them yesterday but not today?"

"Yeah."

"Maybe they are trying to find shelter and can't pick up right now."

Except, when their bodies were found, their phone was gone.

Kate tried her best creating false scenarios, so my mind and heart had something hopeful to cling onto. But somewhere deep in the center of my soul, I felt my tether between my parents snap that night. Like someone took sharp sheers to a sturdy ribbon, fracturing my lifeline, and at that moment, I had never felt so alone.

I used to love the rain.

I only liked it now.

Though every time the sky opened up, it felt like a bittersweet hello from my parents, which was why I didn't hate it.

A warm yellow light glimmered across the bay through the downpour, pulling me from my thoughts. Weston house. My lips turned up as I pictured him sitting on his porch with Masie. I walked to my lamp, squinted, and turned the switch on and off twice. Seconds later, his lights flickered—on, off, on, off.

My cheeks hurt from smiling.

We hadn't seen each other since I found him fixing my dock the other morning. He returned to his regular work schedule, and so had I, meaning I had not left my house in at least a week, and my eyes hurt from staring at my computer screen.

Even though I hadn't seen Weston, I thought about him. He was the only one in this town I could tolerate, and that was saying something. Most of our conversations were superficial. Maybe that was why I enjoyed his company because neither of us had to talk about the one-hundred reasons why everyone else hated us.

Inside our 12,000-square-foot bubble, we were flawless.

I kept it that way by not searching his name, even though my fingers itched to type Weston Turner, APRN, every time I opened a new browser window. I figured if I wanted to get to know him (that was if I wanted to open up too because that was a two-way street), I would do it the right way, not Clifton style.

For now, we'd stay friendly neighbors who occasionally fixed one another docks and attended town meetings together. No distractions.

BY WEDNESDAY EVENING, I was ready to bail on Weston but didn't have his number to call and break the news.

I stood in the middle of my atrocious room, littered with clothes. Nothing matched the occasion, and nothing calmed my nerves. My slow sips of wine—which tasted dryer than a piece of tree bark—turned into a steady gulp, then a second glass.

Today marked the beginning of September, and along came the start of cool evening weather. I settled on a pair of jeans with a short sleeve white tee because I didn't pack much else. I could rummage through my mom's closet, but I was not mentally ready to cross that bridge yet.

Three knocks on my front door sent my head turning. "Shit." He was here. I downed the rest of my drink, grimaced as it washed down my throat, and peeked out of the window to see Weston's car parked in the driveway.

Just like our grocery-store encounter, he wore his work attire, minus the tie and top two buttons. The bags under his eyes were evident but did not take away from his charm. "Hey, you ready to go?" He shoved hands in hidden in his slack pockets.

"You're punctual," I said, glancing at my watch.

"Is that a problem?"

"The three extra minutes from someone late always gives me time to put my shoes on."

"Did you ever stop and think maybe you are the late one?" He looked down at my feet, then past my face at something behind me. "I didn't know we were pre-gaming before this."

I squinted and followed his gaze to the coffee table with the open wine and bottle opener. "Oh, I needed some liquid courage because I don't have any strong sedatives left. Do you prescribe those?"

The corner of his lip raised for a split second, and it took no time for elation to rush through my body, taking shape as a toothy grin on my face. He didn't fully smile, but the tiny ounce of amusement I saw in his expression was enough to satisfy me.

"What time does the meeting start?" he asked.

"At seven. So, that gives us thirty minutes to drive into town, which is usually an eight minutes drive." The tiny amount of alcohol in my veins made me step aside. "You can come in if you'd like and pour a glass of my cheap Cabernet while I put my shoes on."

He kicked his shoes off. "Are we going to be fashionably late?"

"Yes, it won't give anyone a chance to talk to us before the meeting starts."

"Don't worry, nobody will talk to me."

His comment cracked my heart, so I said, "People will talk to me, though, and ask about how my dead parents are doing."

I wasn't in the room to see his reaction to the mention of my parents. Instead, I picked out shoes to wear and finger combed my hair in the mirror. When I returned, Weston observed the photos lining the walls and mantel, holding a normal-sized glass of wine.

"Are these your parents?"

"Yep, the one and only."

We stood side by side, and I wondered what my family looked like from his eyes. He glanced between my face and the picture. "Your hair is lighter here."

"I used to go outside more often."

It was strange to be alone in here with Weston. I expected my parents to come around the corner of their home, asking me to introduce my guest.

"It's strange, you look so much like your dad, but if you look at your mom, you look like her too."

My shoulders bounced with curt laughter. "Yes, Weston, that's how gene expression works."

He looked at me with crinkled eyes. "Sassy tonight, are we? I meant that some people look more like one parent than the other, and you're a perfect blend of both."

"Who do you look like then? Your mom or dad?"

"People always said I look like my mom." And just like that, at the mention of his parents, he shrunk, coiling himself back inside his quiet shell. I wondered if he had lost them from his demeanor but did not ask.

He swallowed the last bit of his drink. "Are we ready to go?"

I groaned.

"That is a no," he said.

"It's not a no. I'm practicing how I'll respond to people when they talk to me."

"Ah, I see."

We trailed to the front door, put our shoes on, and stepped outside so I could lock the house. When I faced the car, the passenger side was open and waiting for me to get in. At the same time, Weston walked around the front of the car and took his place behind the steering wheel.

This was really happening.

I was about to waltz into a town meeting after not being present in Clifton for years. I hadn't shown my face since my parents died two years ago, but even before then, I worked in Oregon, and before that, I was in college. Most, if not all, of the familiar faces I would see tonight had lived here since I was born.

"Can I put the windows down?" I asked as Weston pulled out of my driveway and onto the central road.

"Of course." His voice was flippant.

Before I could press the button, he beat me to it and rolled down all four car windows. The gust of wind lifted my honey-blonde hair, and I held it down before the strands twisted into knots.

The crisp, briny air rid some of my anxiety. Though when the car engine died, and my eyes opened, the reality of the situation came back. I thought the drive was way too short, staring at the large, red brick building.

I could hear the distant thud of boats rocking in the harbor and the sound of crashing waves. The street lamps, adorned with hanging Chrysanthemum baskets, lined the main drag of town and illuminated all of the people bustling inside Town Hall.

This was going to turn into a memorial service. I just knew it.

"Ivey?" Weston's voice snapped me from my daze, and I blinked. "You alright?"

"I'm fine, just a wine headache. Stupid me for getting the cheap stuff." I pushed out of the car and joined Weston around the front with too much sway in my step. My body wobbled, and our hands brushed past one another.

We exchanged looks, then our gaze fell and took in the proximity of our hands. Weston balled his fist, pulling away first. Feeling awkward, I used the same hand to adjust my purse strap.

The inside of Town Hall was just as lively as I thought it would be. People clustered around tables filled with dessert and coffee dispensers. Nobody paid attention as we entered, but one by one, heads turned, and whispering ensued.

Weston leaned in, and my hair shifted as his lips barely scuffed the strands. He whispered, "They're really good at hiding their distaste."

I covered my mouth to laugh.

The cashier, whose name I did not remember, hurried through the throng of people like a bull to a red balloon. "Ivey! You made it." She took my hands, rubbing my knuckles. "And you brought Weston, how kind of you." When she smiled, her eyes squinted so much that I wondered if it hurt.

"He actually brought me. We're happy to be included."

She looped our arms and started walking. I craned my neck, wide-eyed at Weston at her sudden invasion of my personal space. He trailed behind us alone. "It's been so long. Let me introduce you to some folks. Word got around that you would be attending tonight, and I may have told a couple of people," she giggled. "Oh, it's great to have you back. It's like your parents are with us."

My skin burned, and soon enough, we stood before a crowd of people that slowly grew larger. "You guys, remember Ivey Preston? Ester and Logan's daughter." She still hadn't let go of my arm. I listened to the collective gasps and uh-huh's like I was being displayed at a show and tell. Some pity spectacle for everyone to ogle at and pretend they were living vicariously through me.

My replies became autopilot as they bombarded me with questions about my life and my parents. My eyes had trouble focusing on what was in front of me, and I felt myself detaching from the moment. Every hand I shook, I used as a crutch so I would not topple over.

Not everybody in Clifton was inherently bad. There were good people too, but once they got caught in the gossip rip-current, there was no way of getting out. That was the sad part. You couldn't recognize how far out at sea you were until you came up for air.

And, right then and there, I was drowning.

"Is it hard, you know, being in their house?" a woman said.

I felt a hand on my shoulder, a life vest, gently pulling me out of the crowd. "Ivey and I are going to get a coffee before the meeting starts," Weston said, his grip firm and reassuring. I somehow found the power to smile and thank them for the very warm welcome.

They closed the gap I left in their huddle.

Weston's hand moved from my shoulder to the small of my back. His fingers pressed ever-so-gently, guiding me to the refreshment table. If I was in the right state of mind, I would've analyzed the way his touch felt on my skin and filed it in my memory bank of things to recollect when I felt lonely.

"Drink this." He handed me a cup of water. "Slow sips." I listened, and my throat came back to life. "Now I see why you had a couple glasses of wine earlier."

I leaned against the wall, and the temperature of the plaster cooled my body. "I don't think the wine is working in my favor anymore."

He paused. "I don't think this place is working in your favor."

Weston and I were night and day. It was glaringly obvious how much everyone here wanted nothing to do with him. Then there was me; their distaste was not as obvious, but wanting to use me as a pity trophy to pass around was.

"Remind me why we came here again?" I asked, finishing my water.

"I told you to drink that slow." He took my cup and refilled it. "And because we're good locals."

The clamor in the room died down, and I felt the crowd's attention shift to the podium position in front of the chairs. Weston's hand fell to his side, and the muscles in his jaw went rigid as he stared at Clifton's Chief of Staff, Nora Lincoln's, coy smile.

□□□□□□□□❋□□□□□□□□□

QOTD: Do you guys have an Instagram? if so, share your user :) Mine is annasteffeyy

vote • comment • follow

Thanks for reading ♡

□□□□□□□□❋□□□□□□□□□

Chapter 7

Seven | The Secretary

FROM THE COLOR SHIFT IN WESTON'S FACE, it looked like he had seen a ghost, only he was staring at Mrs. Lincoln. What was their story?

"Everyone! Thank you so much for being here and for your patience," the short, black-haired women's voice bellowed into the hall. She clasped her hands together, herding the people like cattle into their chairs. "You all can take your seats."

Weston and I shared a look, then silently trudged to two empty chairs furthest away from the podium and next to the exit in case we needed to make a great escape. What had gotten under his skin? From how he looked at Nora, I knew she had been the culprit of his change in attitude. Why? I would probably never know unless I pried.

"As always, Mayor Wallaby sends his regards. Tonight's meeting has been long awaited. As the autumn season quickly approaches, so does our annual fundraiser for a charity of our choosing."

Collective whispers ensued, and elation sizzled in the air.

"Before we talk about the exciting stuff, we must discuss unpleas-antries." Nora's tonal shift killed the energy in the room like a flick of a switch. People slunk against the backs of their chairs.

If one person was corrupt, it was Nora Lincoln.

Born and raised, just like her predecessors, Nora kept the well-oiled machine that was Clifton functioning. Though the town was still rooted in misogyny, it never elected a woman as Mayor, despite her father and grandfather bearing the position.

Nora did the next best thing and ran for Secretary, which she won, and immediately retitled as Chief of Staff. I had to give her credit; Nora was a force of nature. If everything that came out of her mouth was not backhanded or going to be relayed in a gossip session over coffee, I would look up to her.

She talked about yard upkeep and other nonsense about storing boats for the colder season.

Weston leaned closer. "Do they come and look at our yards?"

I shook my head. "They're probably talking about the houses in town, and our houses are on private driveways in the woods. Al-though, I wouldn't put it past them to come look at ours."

"Now that all the trivial stuff was addressed, it's time to talk about the fundraiser. The council has worked endlessly to find the perfect charity to donate to this year, and we settled on Searching For A Saint in honor of the third anniversary of Ester and Logan Pierce's passing."

My head jerked upright as if someone yanked my hair and forced me to watch the room clap over my dead parents. My nails curled into my palms, stinging. I'm thankful they were blunt, or else I would've penetrated my skin.

This had to be a joke.

Nora touched her hand to her heart. "We have the privilege of having Ivey Pierce, their only daughter, back in town to celebrate with us." She droned on about how Searching For A Saint was a non-profit organization that helped locate missing people, and it was only "fitting" because my parents were missing for forty hours before being found.

People faced me, clasping their hands like in prayer, and smiled pitifully. I gnawed on the inside of my cheek, casting tight-lipped half-smiles in their direction. They were being nice, I told myself. Not everyone was out to get you; this wasn't a ploy to dig up your trauma.

But it felt that way, and my mind struggled to distinguish my thoughts from reality. All I knew was I needed to get out of this building, needed the eyes off of me, and heaps of fresh air because my lungs were running on fumes.

Nora talked about how September would be their preparation month when Weston gripped the back of my chair. "Come on, we're leaving."

"I can't just get up and walk out of here."

"You can do whatever you want, Ivey."

I pinched the bridge of my nose, trying to alleviate the budding pressure. I needed to wait this out, and the last thing I wanted was to draw attention to myself. "We will go when she stops talking," I said.

He listened, moving his hand back into his lap without protest. And for the next fifteen minutes, we did just that, listen to the babbling around us. The second Nora stopped, everyone stood for another round of refreshments, and Weston and I booked it to his car and sped down the road before anyone could stop us.

I sat with my hands clasped against my thighs. My heart rate had significantly slowed to tolerable drumming, yet my body felt worn down.

"What was that back there?" Weston finally broke the silence.

"Welcome to Clifton."

I felt him look at me but didn't meet his gaze. I was mortified and overwhelmed, and the last thing I wanted to do was explain how my plan for tonight went entirely south—not that I even had a solid plan. I just wanted to show my face and hope that bygones were bygones, but it seemed like everyone was still hung up over my parent's death, even more than I was.

A fundraiser? Really? A fucking fundraiser?

"I know a panic attack when I see one, and I watched you have two in an hour."

"No need to diagnose me, Mr. APRN," I laughed, trying to lighten the mood. Though, it was killed long ago.

I had learned to cope with panic attacks (I thought I had them wrangled at least) but tonight showed me how powerful my emotions were and how fast they can change.

"You can't control the actions of others," my father would tell me. "You can only control how you react."

I rested my head on the window, ridding the memories from my mind. I didn't want to think about them anymore tonight.

"Do you want to talk about any of it?" Weston asked.

"What about the little reaction you had to Nora Lincoln?"

"Did I react? I didn't realize I did."

I analyzed his face, but no wrinkle or expression hinted toward an answer to my question. So, we were both unwilling to open up tonight, which was okay since I did not have the energy. Maybe one day, I would tell him all the unpleasant thoughts running through my head.

Weston made a right down my long driveway. The moonlight cascaded through the leaves, and white shadows danced on my lap. The light above the front door was the only thing illuminating the land. It looked eerily vacant, especially with the vines I had yet to pull off the house.

"I'm sorry tonight wasn't very fun," he said as if it was his fault.

I laughed heartily as I climbed out and rested my elbows on the windowsill, looking back at Weston seated in the driver's seat. "It's not your fault, Wes. I thought it would be fun to watch everyone bicker over stupid, meaningless shit, but I wasn't expecting my family to be the subject of every conversation."

"You just have to tell them to fuck off."

My eyes bulged from their sockets. "Woah, I never thought I'd hear the word fuck out of your mouth."

"Then you've got a lot to learn about me, Ivey," he jeered, and the corner of my mouth softly curled up. "Goodnight."

"Night." He drove off, the dust sputtering behind his tires, and floated around the red tail lights until he was fully out of sight. I sat on the brick stoop staring into the darkness until I mustered the courage to go inside.

Two wine glasses stood tall on the coffee table, stained red from not being rinsed out. I kicked off my shoes, threw my purse on the couch, and then opened the porch doors to let the cool air percolate through the muggy space.

I picked both stems up with one hand, the bottle in the other, and carried them to the sink.

Besides the clinking of dishes and running water, I let the sounds from outside fill my body until my nerves weren't humming with anxiety. The ambient noise was exactly what I needed to rid my head of Nora's speech tonight.

But soon enough, I finished cleaning and found myself standing in front of the den doors where years of my parent's research lived. I had yet to go inside because I knew I would find the project they were working on that led to their demise. My therapist had strongly suggested I skimmed their research as a part of my healing journey, but I never came back here to try.

My lungs burned from holding my breath as I reached for the door handle and pushed inside.

A large mahogany desk sat in the center of the room. Books and papers were strewn across the top underneath an antique Bankers Lamp. Dad always said the green lamp shade was good for setting the mood. The leather armchair was pulled out as though it had just been used, and someone forgot to push it back under the desk.

Like the living room, bookshelves and windows lined the walls, two of which faced the backyard and the others faced the side of the house, just like I remembered.

I tiptoed over and stared at the papers on the desk. Drawings of plants, shells, trees, and animals came into view, and each was signed with my mother's name and labeled Clifton Bay.

Were they working on a book about Clifton? Sitting on the edge of the chair, I sifted through the papers in astonishment. My parents never researched here because they didn't want our home life to become a job, even though their job interfered with our lives more times than I could count.

Though, I admired their sentiment.

Before my curiosity kept me up all night, I decided it was time for bed.

I locked the porch doors and turned off the house lights. Before I wandered to my bedroom, Weston's porch lights caught my attention. On, off, on, off.

My heart swelled at the unexpected, late-night salutation. I turned my light on once in greeting and waited, but Wes's lights never turned back.

I took the hint and trekked to my bedroom, undressing as I walked.

I climbed under my chilly sheets, only in my underwear, unable to bring myself to shower. The weight of today hung over me like heavy storm clouds. I let them spill, and cried myself to sleep.

❏❏❏❏❏❏❏❏✿❏❏❏❏❏❏❏❏

Did you guys see the map I made for Clifton? If you didn't I attached it below :)

QOTD: If you had a superpower, what would it be?

vote • comment • follow

Thanks for reading ♡

❏❏❏❏❏❏❏❏✿❏❏❏❏❏❏❏❏

Chapter 8

Eight | Chores

THE BOAT HUMMED BENEATH my body as I glided through the bay.

After letting my frigid fingers drag in the wake, I dried them and watched the land pass in hasty blurs of green. When I spotted the tiny inland Marldec overflowing with foliage, I pulled back on the break, and the boat slowed.

I climbed out of bed this morning, clear-eyed and driven by my newfound curiosity, even after last night.

My parents didn't tell me they were working on a local journal, and I wasn't sure why it bothered me. Did they not feel like Clifton was their home anymore? Or was I thinking too deeply about it?

After getting ready, I shoved the papers and journals on Clifton from my parent's desk into a bag, poured myself a heaping travel mug of coffee, filled the tank of the motorboat in our boat garage, and took her onto the water. My hair immediately turned to frizzy waves.

My boat thudded against a mud bank, and my rain boots sank into the soft earth as I held onto the side of the boat to find my balance.

The ground made a schlooppp sound as I yanked each foot out, shook mud from my shoes, and then began searching the area.

The trees were dense, except there was no sun for them to protect me from; instead, it was murky and cool in the shade.

My mother's sketches were marked with locations in the corner alongside the date she found them with my father. My parents were old school, so a polaroid was taped in the corner with every sketch. But that was their style. All their published journals were unique enough that if you saw a page from their book, you knew it was Logan and Ester Pierce's work.

When I located the same plants labeled in their sketchbook, I took pictures with my Canon camera and continued until all the plants from this area were accounted for and stored on my SD card. Then, I hopped back in my boat and headed home.

I was still determining why I went to the island in the first place, considering I was too busy with work from Larry to take on the burden of a random project my parents were working on. Though, picking up where they left off made me feel like I was a part of their crew.

I veered to the left, and my boat drifted back toward my house.

The sharp sound of metal on metal echoed off the water, and Weston, hunched over, came into sight. His boat bobbed beside my dock, and Masie sat beside him as he hammered away.

He was back.

I cupped my hands around my mouth. "You're trespassing!"

Weston stood up straight and rested his hammer over his shoulder. "You have a boat?"

"This ol' thing?" I patted the port side where the name 'Little Bird' was chipping away. "It's my parents," I said, drifting past him and into the garage hidden by vines and overgrown tree branches, then made my way back down the dock on foot.

"It's a Thursday, aren't you supposed to be at the office?" Masie pressed against my legs, wanting her back scratched. I used my nails to itch above her leg, never taking my eyes off Weston.

"I'm on call today. No appointments were scheduled, so I told Lisa, my secretary, to take the day off."

"So you're spending your day off fixing my dock at six in the morning?"

He just shrugged. "What were you doing out that early on your boat? Getting rid of a dead body?"

"Yeah, people come trespassing, and I take them out like Dexter."

He covered his eyes. "I didn't see a thing."

I laughed once and hung my feet over the edge, and my boots barely grazed the water's surface. Masie followed. The cold exterior that radiated from Weston was slowly turning lukewarm. His shoulders weren't as stiff, and his jaw wasn't as rigid as he was constantly holding back a fuck-you monologue.

He still hadn't fully smiled, teeth and all. I waited for the day he would.

"Wes—" I gathered his attention even though I already had it. He paused, and the hammer hovered above the nail, waiting for me to continue. "What do you call a fish wearing a bowtie?" I asked, and he raised his brow. "So-fish-ticated." I enunciated the word, then burst into fake laughter, slapping my leg.

"You are so strange," he said, without total disgust—that's a start.

"Admit it was good."

"If you were a dad of six, yeah."

"Jeesh, tough crowd."

He continued hammering, and a breeze rustled the tops of the trees and sputtered across the water, causing tiny ripples in the surface. The clouds still hadn't cracked, and they grew darker and released a low grumble.

"A storm is brewing." Just as the words left my mouth, rain pelted us inconsistently. Masie took off without warning toward my house just when lightning illuminated the black sky. Weston shouted for her, trying to collect his tools simultaneously.

"I've got her. Meet us in the house!" My camera bag bounced against my back.

I usually entered through the mud room. I would never trudge through the house in my muddy rain boots, yet, Masie leaned against the porch door on the steps, trying to fit her chubby body under the tiny awning.

"Here you go, girl," I said like she understood, opening the door. She ran to the corner of the screened room, spun around three times, and then settled on the floor with her chin resting on her paws. She licked her lips loudly, content.

"Is that better?" I chuckled.

I walked outside as Weston approached. "Masie's in here. You guys can wait out the storm here if you want."

He nodded, and I told him I would take my boots off around the front. Moments later, with my shoes in the mud-room sink, I met him on the porch as the rain fell in heaps.

"It's really coming down."

"Yeah, it is. The radar didn't call for a storm, though." He scratched his chin.

"That's the beauty of living on the coast. Can I get you coffee or tea?"

"Coffee would be great," he said. "And a towel, if it's not too much to ask?"

I saw his rain-soaked shirt and sopping-wet hair and internally scolded myself for not offering first.

"Of course." I dashed to the linen closet and grabbed a perfectly folded towel that had not been touched in years. "The bathroom is across from the staircase, and I'll be in the kitchen."

Weston didn't know that the tiny hallway beside the staircase leading to the kitchen had a perfect view of the bathroom. This house was built in the late 1700s when hidden hallways and secret doors were built into homes to hide staff from guests. The idea of it all was terrible, but my younger self loved the maze-like floor plan.

And now, I loved it even more because I had a perfect view of Weston, who left the bathroom door open. He yanked his shirt off, drying his chest and arms, then moved to his brown hair, which had become curlier from the humidity and rain. Then, he shook out his tee with the towel draped over his shoulders.

I squinted and really looked at him.

He was attractive, not just in looks but in how he carried himself. He didn't peg me as a nice guy at first, though, but nobody commits random acts of service if you aren't kind deep down. It took a beat for him to warm up to me and my sarcastic mouth.

He still hadn't brought up the last night's disaster, and I hoped he would not.

The coffee sputtered into a mug. "Do you need me to toss your shirt in the dryer?"

"No, it should be okay. Thanks."

When I looked back, he was gone. My forehead wrinkled, and I carried both mugs into the living room. Weston's teeshirt was back on while he glanced at the books lining the shelves. Damn.

"Are these your parents?"

I handed his mug to him. "Some of them, yeah."

"How many do they have?"

"About thirteen published."

"Wow." He pulled out one about South Carolina that they had written when I was six. Dust lifted into the air and flipped through the pages filled with drawings and descriptions. "These are incredible."

I smiled, proud of their work, even though it made my heart ache.

He tucked the book back in its spot. We meandered to the living room couches, sitting opposite one another, and I pulled my feet up and tucked them under my body. Masie found us and curled beside Weston's feet as the storm raged on.

"So, Searching For A Saint?" he eyed me, sipping his coffee. This was the most he's ever talked and the longest I had ever stayed quiet. I heaved a sigh, not wanting to think about last night.

Assuming Weston's already looked up what happened to my parents, I said, "I swear this town has always exploited their death."

"Have you confronted them?"

"I only just got back. I haven't lived here for nine years and didn't stay after their funeral."

"I thought you said you lived here for nineteen years?"

"I was born and raised in Clifton but left after high school."

"Ah," he said, finally understanding. "I see why you left."

"Yeah. Why'd you come here?"

It was his turn to sigh. "A job opening."

"The good ol' job vortex. It'll suck you right in."

He snorted. "How about you? Why'd you come back?"

The almighty question.

I sank into the cushions as if they could protect me, taking my time nursing down a mouthful of coffee before answering. "I came back to figure out what to do with this house." I motioned around me. "I hadn't been back since their passing, and it has been sitting here collecting dust. I know I either need to sell it or do something with the place because, even though this sounds terrible, the thought of it bound to my name, just sitting here kind of prolongs me from moving on with my life."

I looked around as if the walls had an answer to my dilemma.

"I don't think that sounds terrible."

I was ready to contradict him and explain how most people told me it sounded terrible, but in reality, nobody had ever said those words because I had never asked. The only thing convincing me my thoughts were horrible was my festering subconscious which did not seem to be on my side.

"I guess I feel terrible about it."

"That sounds a lot like grief talking." I met his gaze, surprised by his reply, and he quickly added, "Sorry, I didn't mean to say that."

"No, no, you're probably right. It is much harder to discern the grieving process when you are in it, even though I have no trouble pointing it out to others.

He nodded, and the conversation drifted on.

He didn't ask about the ghastly details of my parent's death. He didn't press any further for rationales for my decisions or question why I was still poorly grieving after two years. I did not even know why. Maybe I shouldn't have left therapy so early.

Instead, we talked about Masie, even though I wanted to ask him other questions. Why was he here in Clifton, and if it was genuinely job-driven, what his business with Nora Lincoln was, or what he did do—if he did anything—for the town to hate him so damn much.

When we were done with our coffee, he followed me to the kitchen, and his eyes nearly fell from their sockets. "Ivey Pierce, you let your dishes pile up?"

"Okay listen," I began to explain myself. "You know how we all have that one chore we really hate? Like deeply despise? Mine is doing the dishes," I say, and he gapes. "I know it's gross, but now since you've seen my dark secret, you have to tell me yours."

"I don't have any. I'm perfect."

"Ha ha, Turner. Very funny," I said, even though part of me believed him.

The corner of his mouth curled upward in a grin. The sight of his good mood did something to my insides, considering the drumming in my chest sounded like a marching band at half-time.

Weston laid the hand towel from the oven door on the counter and turned the facet on. My face heated. "Are you going to do the dishes? Oh God, please don't."

"What are all these plants on the table?" he ignored me.

I propped myself on a stool, staring at the back of his head. He moved with ease, sudsing the handful of porcelain dishes that had acclimated over the days. I wished his tee shirt wasn't black because I could barely see the outline of his back muscles underneath.

"For work," I said because it was the most straightforward answer, and it was not technically a lie.

"What do you do?"

"Well, I have my Ph.D. in biology, but I also double majored in botany. I travel and research certain areas in the United States, but right now, I'm taking a break to be here."

"Wow, Ivey. That's impressive."

I chuckled, feeling weary in accepting the compliment. "I'm lucky to travel for work."

"So what are you working on now?" he asked, and just when I was about to answer, he said, "Are you gonna sit there, or are you going to dry?"

My jaw fell open, and a curt laugh slipped out. "I can dry, but we use our words to ask for help here, Weston." I snapped back, picked a fresh towel from the drawer, and dried the dishes, setting them in their respective cabinets.

I told Weston all about Larry and the project I was working on with my best friend, Kate, and I didn't mention the journals I found in my parent's office, why I was out on the boat this morning, or how most of my major life decisions revolved around pleasing my parents. And now that they were gone who the hell was there to please?

"So nobody else in your family could come and get the house ready for you?"

"My parents were the flower children who ran off and did their own thing, and I was told what little family I have is scattered throughout the states. We never talked to them, and as far as I'm aware, they probably don't know I exist."

"Do they know your parents passed?"

I shrugged. "I didn't know who anyone was, so I couldn't reach out and tell them. The only person who knows is my mom's sister, but she is off in Europe traveling now."

He paused and met my gaze.

The water ran onto his motionless hands while he watched me. The last thing I wanted was pity from Weston, and I could feel it oozing out of him now.

"Don't worry," I smiled, drying the last dish. "I'm a big girl."

Harsh ringing echoed into the room, pulling us from our staring contest. Weston dried his hands off and tugged his phone from his pocket. I watched every ounce of happiness drain from his face as he answered. "Hello? Yeah, I'll be there in 10 minutes. Thanks for calling. Bye."

"You have to go in?"

"Yeah."

"Do you want me to drive you back to your place?"

"You don't have to."

"Seriously? You just washed my dishes; it's the least I can do. Come on."

He didn't fight me, instead called Masie over, and we all piled into my car, trying to avoid getting wetter. When I pulled up to the blue house—which I had never been this close to—he thanked me.

Just before he closed the door to the car, he leaned back in, the rain pounding against his back. "Can I ask a huge favor?"

"Uh, sure."

"Would you mind watching Masie for me on Monday?"

I looked at his front door, where Masie patiently waited to go inside. "Of course, I can watch her."

"I'll text you!" he shouted over the thunder and was just about to slam the door.

"Wait! I don't have your number!"

He handed his phone to me, and I speedily typed my number into a new contact, watching him get soaked. The cool gusts of wind blowing into the car did nothing to the warmth that sizzled through my body; if anything, I grew hotter.

Then, he said goodbye for real and hurried into his house as I drove back to mine.

□□□□□□□□❀□□□□□□□□

Hi guys, sorry it's been a bit. I began my ICU rotation/clinical (a uni class) at the hospital and I've been so busy studying, I haven't had much time to write. I hope you enjoy this chapter, I'm excited to share more.

QOTD: Do you like thunderstorms? If so, what is your favorite thing to do during them?

vote • comment • follow

Thanks for reading ♡

□□□□□□□□❀□□□□□□□□

Chapter 9

Nine | Wet Dog

MY PHONE RANG at five-thirty in the morning. I slammed my hand on the dresser where it lay and pulled it to my ear. "Hello?"

"Hi, I'm at your front door."

Every nerve ending lit up as I sprang forward. "What?"

"I have Masie with me."

My toes curled against the hardwood as I climbed out of bed and ran around the room in nothing but underwear and a tee shirt, frantically looking for my misplaced robe. When it didn't appear out of thin air, I settled on wrapping myself in my blanket and hiked toward the door.

The sky could've been mistaken for the night when I opened the door and saw Weston standing with Masie on a leash. Even in the dark, he looked good in his navy blue button-up and slacks. His hair was neatly fixed, unlike mine.

He observed me and then teasingly said, "Morning, sunshine."

I narrowed my eyes. "Morning."

"Sorry for waking you up."

"You go in this early?"

"Just today."

I rubbed my eyes, trying not to get too close since I hadn't brushed my teeth. Although I didn't mind, I did not know why he needed me to watch Masie when he had been leaving her alone every other day.

He handed me a small bag of food and her bowl. "Thanks again. I have some extra things to do today, so I won't be home until a little later. Is that okay?"

"That's fine by me." I took Masie's leash and crouched to pet her. She was just as lethargic as me, leaning into my body to support her sleepy weight. I rubbed her head.

"You be good for Ivey, May. I'll text you later."

We locked eyes, not saying anything else before the door closed, separating us. I set Masie's food bowl down, filled up some water for her to drink, and then walked back to my bedroom and fell asleep until the sun poured through my blinds around eight.

When I woke, Masie was sprawled out on the floor beside my bed. Her belly expanded and contracted in a steady rhythm, and her lips flapped when she exhaled. I chuckled, brushing my unkept hair from my eyes.

"Good morning Masie," I called out. "Guess what we're doing today? We're getting some work done for Larry, then going on an adventure."

After my morning coffee and working on more of my column for the magazine assignment, I changed into an outfit more appropriate for hiking, threw my backpack with my camera, a water bottle, and

Masie's water bowl. Right before I left the house, I ran into the office and grabbed my parent's journal from their desk.

The weather was a perfect blend of summer and fall. The sun's rays were powerful enough to keep me warm despite the biting breeze, especially on the boat. I knew I would start sweating once we were under the sun long enough.

Masie climbed into the boat quickly. I didn't have a dog life vest, so I macgyvered a human vest to fit her since we were going far and I did not want to risk her falling out.

The engine hummed to life, and we sailed toward the Marsh Lands west of Clifton.

Masie's ears flapped in the wind as her body bounced at the bow with each wave. Almost ten minutes later, we drifted toward brambles of trees and sandy dunes covered in thick wads of beach grass. They leaned sideways from the constant battering breeze blowing off the water.

I craned my head around and back on land and saw the Lincoln property peeking through the trees. I pursed my lips, trying to avoid thinking about the history between Nora and Weston, and kept pushing forward.

Turning left, I looped around the marsh to find where my parents used to dock the boat. There was no harbor, just skid marks in the earth and a makeshift post where I could tie the ropes.

The closer we got to land and the slower my boat became, the more I could hear the hidden cicadas singing under the dense weeping willows and bald cypress trees.

Masie stood up, wagging her tail at the sight of solid earth.

"Ah! Sit," I shouted. She listened, though her tail still showed excitement.

We spent the next two hours hiking and boating to different spots in the marshes. I followed my mother's drawings, taking pictures of everything I could find. Mixed between all of the nature photos were portraits of Masie.

"Masie! Hey, girl!" I called as she trailed in front of me.

She would pause, turn her head with her teeth and tongue out, panting, and I would snap the photo. Who knew a dog could be so photogenic? But she was perfect, and each picture looked like a still from a catalog. I was confident Weston would love these photos, so I made a mental note to send them to him later.

The further we walked, the filthier we got, and I would have to give her a bath before giving her back because the poor girl's legs and belly were covered in thick mud.

For a brief moment, I pictured what it would be like if it was Weston, Masie, and me.

I hadn't anticipated coming back to Clifton and making a friend (Kate would call Weston otherwise), but it felt nice knowing I could talk with him and not have to pretend.

Later in the day, after lunch, Masie and I walked through town along the harbor. I could see Weston's practice through the row of trees lining the sidewalk, and I wondered if Masie knew he was close. If she did, she didn't care and trotted along.

It had grown considerably hotter as the day progressed, and we were both in desperate need of a drink. So, we walked to Oliver's Cafe, where I stood in line to get water for Masie and an iced coffee for me.

Rocking on my heels, I stared at Weston's contact and wondered if he wanted a coffee.

When I got to the counter, the cashier's eyes widened. "Ivey? As in Ivey Pierce?" They looked excited while I tried to mask my confusion.

I took in her light pink Hijab and big brown eyes, and then it hit me. It was Maram Nadar. She was ten years older than the last time I saw her in high school. She was a grade above me, so we weren't close, but she was the head of the high-school paper and best friends with Zoe Lincoln, Nora Lincoln's only child.

"Maram! Wow, I almost didn't recognize you."

"Same to you, except I had heard your name around town and wondered when I would run into you. How are you? How long have you been back?"

I blew air through pursed lips, feeling comfortable enough to talk with her. "Almost a month now, and I'm doing alright. What about you?"

"It's so nice to see your face again." She paused and cast a warm smile. "And I'm great, thanks. What can I get you?"

I ordered, then followed her down the length of the counter. We both small-talked as she made my drink. To my surprise, I learned she married the owner of Oliver's Cafe, who took over the business after his father passed. I should've noticed the large rock on her ring finger.

It was strange to see people from high school older and married to people we graduated with. Because in my mind, we're all 15, running around town and swimming in the ocean without care. Now we had the weight of life on our shoulders.

Maram handed me our beverages and then leaned over the counter to look at the sleepy Saint Bernard. "And who might this muddy fella be?"

"This is Masie." I rubbed her head.

Maram stared at Masie, then backed up at me and cast a smile that didn't reach her eyes. What did that look mean? Her gaze lingered on me, then she clasped her hands together and said we should catch up again before saying goodbye. I agreed and headed for a seat closest to the door, wanting to be in the air conditioning longer. Masie curled up overtop my feet.

"They're assigning tasks for the fundraiser tomorrow night," a woman sitting near me spoke.

"Did you hear Zoe is coming back to town? Nora is totally stressing over it. Did you see how she acted at our book club meeting the other night? She practically drank half a bottle of wine."

"Why? Because of the practitioner?"

The pressure in my head grew the wider my eyes got. Practitioner? As in Weston? I listened, waiting to hear more, but I didn't. Without turning my head, I glanced at the women in my periphery.

"He was at the last meeting with the Pierce girl. He is making his rounds, and I wonder who he'll move onto next when she leaves."

"How do you know she's leaving?"

"Come on." The woman's short cackle echoed into the space. "That girl doesn't belong here, and there are rumors she's selling the manor."

"I would kill to have that house, and it baffles me a 27-year-old inherited it and then let it rot for two years."

My heart pounded so hard it hurt. I wondered if this was the closest feeling to a heart attack. Would they be talking this way if they knew I was sitting right here, or did they already know I was listening and that was their goal?

"Do you think she knows Turner was with Zoe?"

Now my heart was lodged in my throat.

"Who knows."

The topic of their conversation shifted. Thankfully this one did not concern Weston or me. I didn't want to draw attention to myself, so I waited a couple of minutes before hurrying out of the cafe, past Weston's office toward home, wondering what the hell I had just heard.

"COME ON, MASIE, I need to wash you before your dad gets home," I pleaded, trying to lift her into the giant plastic kitty pool I used to play in, which I found in the garage and filled with hot water.

She fought me, barking loud while I almost threw my back out, placing her in the water. "You'll survive."

I settled on washing her with Dawn Soap since I didn't have any animal shampoo and according to the internet, using human shampoo was not a good idea, and I was not going to be the one to mess up Weston's dog's fur.

The music carried from my phone speaker into the room. The sun had set entirely, lending day to night.

I hadn't heard from Weston once, and all I could think about was the conversation I had overheard in the cafe.

Weston didn't have a history with Nora Lincoln. He had one with Zoe. And from what I could tell, it was intimate. Was it a fling? Were they still seeing each other? I laughed out loud at how bizarre my thoughts were. I cared more about the gossip I heard about Weston than the terrible things those women said about me.

How sad.

Needing to vent and hear my best friend's voice, I dried my hands off and called Kate. She answered on the second ring.

"Hey, I've." I could hear her excitement. "I was just thinking about you."

"I must've felt it because I was thinking about you too."

"Even across the country, we're connected."

"Always. I miss you. How was your week?"

We spent most of our call catching up about our week and work. I was ecstatic to hear what she had been up to, but the stories made my stomach clench with homesickness. My everyday life felt so out of reach when I was here.

Masie barked when I poured water down her back.

"Was that a dog?" Kate asked.

"I'm dog-sitting."

"You're dog-sitting? For who?"

"Weston," I admitted hesitantly.

"You mean your hot neighbor nurse? Ivey, what the hell!"

"He had work and errands to run, so I agreed to watch her. I'm giving her a bath because we hiked through the marshlands today and got dirty." After I explained, I wondered what errands he was talking about.

"The next thing you know, he's gonna ask if you can babysit him too."

My shoulders bounced with laughter. "Kate, that is so—"

Three loud knocks reverberated through the house, instantly sending Masie into a frenzy. "Kate, I have to go!" I screamed, and before I could stop her, the Saint Bernard jumped out of the tub, and I body slammed the ground, trying to hold her still.

"Masie! Come!" I shouted, watching her run into the house drenched. Then, as I pushed myself slowly from the floor, I realized I was also drenched with the muddy bath water.

"Ivey! What the hell is going on?" Weston's voice came from the foyer.

"I-uh," I stood up, grabbed the towel that was supposed to be for the dog, and covered my see-through shirt. I followed the water trail throughout the house, holding Masie's collar.

Weston was crouching beside his pet, staring up at me in horror. His perplexed expression—which eyed me up and down—slowly turned into the most prominent, radiant smile I have ever seen.

He tipped his head back, and the silence was filled with pure laughter.

Weston Turner was laughing and smiling; it was the most beautiful sight.

My body heated to an unhealthy temperature, and I half expected my wet skin to begin evaporating dry.

"What the hell happened? Why are you both so wet? Did you fall in the bay?"

I pinched the bridge of my nose, trying to cover my breast that most definitely were visible through my tee-shirt. "We went to the marshland today, and she was covered in mud, and I thought I'd give her a bath. She heard your knocking... and now here we are."

His smile stretched ear to ear as he looked between Masie and me. "Well, that's very kind of you. Thank you."

His eyes flickered to my sheer shirt, then back to my face. Or was that my lips he looked at? Oh, God.

"Will you take her back to the mudroom, please?" I pointed in the direction behind me, needing a moment to collect myself. "I'm going to change."

"Sure."

When I got to my bathroom, I gripped the granite countertop for support and to steady my breath, unsure of what overcame me. I never thought I would see him smile or laugh like that or that I would react that way.

My face was beet red, and it looked like I had laid under the sun for hours without sunscreen. I stood straight, staring at my round nipples prodding through my shirt, trying to picture myself through Weston's eyes.

Was this how he saw me? I turned from side to side, smoothing my hands over my top.

Why did I suddenly care?

Distracting myself, I stripped and threw on something dry, pulling my half-wet hair back in a clip. When I returned to the mud room, Weston's white shirt sleeves were rolled up, exposing his muscular forearms, and he knelt beside the tub Masie was back inside.

"Finishing what I started," I said, kneeling on the floor to wipe the water trail.

"You did the leg work. I'm just rinsing the rest of the soap out."

He looked at me, and we both smiled at each other. I felt that same pull inside of me that I had felt earlier.

"How was your day? Get everything you needed to get done?"

He shrugged. "It was fine, and I got things done. How about you?"

"It was also fine." Aside from the gossip session I overheard, I wasn't ready to tell him about that.

"You guys went on an adventure then?"

"Yes, we did, and we had a lot of fun. I have photos to show you."

"She was good for you?"

"Yes, she was great company too."

We continued working in comfortable silence. Everything I wanted to say stayed tucked inside my head, safe and sound. I was not ready to hear about Zoe Lincoln. So, I mopped while he dried Masie off and poured the dirty water outside.

"So, I was thinking," I started, out of the blue. "I may go to the town meeting again this week."

His nose wrinkled. "You really wanna subject yourself to that again?"

"I mean..." I thought of what to reply. "I figured getting in everyone's good graces would be best."

"Why, though? They're assholes, and they don't deserve your kindness."

My shoulders bobbed, despite my heart skipping a beat from his indirect compliment. "I don't know."

He stared at me for an uncomfortable amount of time. I could tell he was trying to read my demeanor, but I didn't let anything show. When he didn't find what he was looking for, he sighed. "Well, I'm not letting you go alone, so I'll pick you up Wednesday."

"Oh, I did not mean to make you feel forced—"

"I don't."

It was my turn to analyze his face, but all I imagined was his beautiful smile from early and the sound of his amusement.

"Okay, well, don't feel obliged to come. If you bail, I'll be fine."

He took one step closer to me. "I do not bail, Ivey."

"Okay," was all I could squeak out.

Without hesitating, his thumb brushed my cheekbone, and my breath stalled in my throat. "You've still got mud on your face, and I think it's your turn for a shower."

He was looking at me how every woman wants to be looked at by a man. And just like that, in a split second, I felt the meaning of our relationship shift into something I didn't quite understand.

Nevertheless, I had a knack for overanalyzing the simplest of things, including meaningless gestures, which was what precisely happened.

This was one of those self-sabotaging moments where I could make or break a friendship.

"Uh, yeah," I choked. "I smell like a wet dog. I should go do that."

He thanked me again for watching Masie and left me in the foyer. The walls around me felt tight, and the air felt thick. Yet, for some reason, I hoped he would think about me tonight when he fell asleep.

□□□□□□□□✿□□□□□□□□

;)

QOTD: What was the most recent movie you saw? Did you enjoy it?

vote • comment • follow

Thanks for reading ♡

□□□□□□□□✿□□□□□□□□

Chapter 10
Ten | Motherly Instinct

WESTON DID NOT break his promise and bail on me. At six-forty-five, he knocked on my front door while I slipped on my shoes and prepared to attend the place I knew would put me in a foul mood.

"We're not wine-pregaming?" the displeasure in his voice was evident.

I pulled locked the front door behind me. "Nope, not tonight."

"You sure you wanna go? It is not too late to back out."

"Did you say blackout? That wasn't on our list of things to do tonight, but I'll consider changing plans."

He released one short laugh, and my cheeks immediately turned crimson from the sound. Another laugh. This was new, and it was an advancement. I wasn't sure what had changed within him in the last two days, but I didn't mind his sparse smiles and laughter.

Nevertheless, I could not pretend I was going to this meeting solely for myself or out of the kindness of my heart.

I couldn't get Zoe Lincoln out of my head since I overheard the two women talking in the cafe. She and Wes had a history, not that it was any of my business, and I was curious how their relationship went south enough for the whole town to shun him.

It seemed people were associating us together now, which I didn't mind, but it was not like we were romantically involved. He wasn't making his rounds. Hell, the guy smiled at me for the first time in three weeks.

However, Zoe was an entirely different story.

She was the only child of the Lincolns, and Nora was nothing short but protective over her only daughter. Unlike her mother, Zoe was kind and soft-spoken in high school and was favored by default because of her family's status.

I hadn't known Zoe well, but she and Wes seemed like an odd pairing, and how they knew each other was beyond me.

I watched him in my periphery, his fingers drumming on the steering wheel to some radio song. His head bobbed along, too, barely noticeable, and my heart hastened.

At that moment, I must've looked at him too long and closely because I saw an entirely different man sitting beside me.

The lines on his face were soft. His tired eyes, having seen so much sickness, were also gentle. The rigid, reserved man I met on my dock and in the doctor's office was nowhere to be seen. Was this the true Wes? Was there a genuine version of myself I had yet to show him, or had he already seen me?

I gulped deep breaths when we pulled into the lot. Thanks to the adrenaline and preparation I had before coming, I was not nearly as anxious as the last meeting. I knew I would hear about my dead parents tonight, so I put my game face on.

"If you wanna leave at any point, just give me a look, and we can go," he said, following the flock inside.

"Alright."

People were not as overwhelming with their greetings; they kept their hands to themselves and didn't pull me in different directions. I stayed at Weston's side most of the night, talking with residents about how I was 'looking forward to the fundraiser' even though that was a lie.

I spotted Maram and Oliver by the refreshment table.

She eagerly waved. However, when her eyes coasted to my right where Weston stood, her smile faltered, then returned to normal before anyone could notice. But I noticed. If anyone knew details about what happened between Zoe and Weston, it would be Maram, considering she was best friends with Zoe in high school.

I walked toward her, and Weston trailed behind.

"Hey, Maram."

"Hey, it's wonderful to see you here."

She reintroduced me to Oliver Jr., then I motioned to Weston. "You've met Weston Turner, right? He's the new nurse practitioner in town."

I watch their interaction as if I were inspecting it under a microscope. They shook hands, Maram could barely keep complete eye contact, and Weston seemed like he didn't have a clue as to what was going on. I could not tell if her indifference was like everyone else's—just because the town agreed to feel that way—or because she knew more than she was letting on.

"How'd you two meet?" Oliver asked, oblivious to the tension.

"We're neighbors. He lives in Mr. Morris's old house."

Their mouths formed an O-shape in understanding.

"How are you liking it here in Clifton?" Maram directed the question toward Wes.

He put an entirely different front for Maram, smiling and all. It was like I was watching someone new altogether. "It's an adjustment compared to the city, but nice and quiet."

So he's from the city... I realized I really knew nothing about him.

"You know what? We should totally double date!" Maram's excitement was evident, and Weston and I glanced at each other, realizing she mistook us for a couple. He opened his mouth, but I was already correcting her before he could speak.

"We're not a couple, but dinner would be nice as a group."

"Oh! My mistake." She shook her head, holding her hands up in defense. I did everything in my power to prevent my brows from furrowing, and I never could tell if anyone in this damned town was genuine.

Those "mistakes" screamed deliberate. I could care less if Maram was being nosey, though my genuine concern was if her questions were ill-intended. I'm sure the whole town will know we're not a couple by tomorrow, which, I guess, settles rumors—if there were any, to begin with.

Nora walked to the podium, grabbing everyone's attention and people took their seats. For once, Mayor Wallaby came, greeting his residents with one hand over his rotund belly and the other waving in the air.

While they spoke, Weston leaned over. "I'm way too sober for this."

I stifled a laugh. "Same. You were right, and we should've pre-gamed."

He shrugs, his lips pursed together in an I-told-you-so expression.

Nora's voice bellowed. "As you know, tonight, we are assigning roles in preparation for the fundraiser at the end of this month. Remember, guests come from inland to celebrate every year, and we need to show them how amazing and special it is to live in Clifton. You are all the stars of the show, so make sure you shine."

I think I heard Weston gag. "I thought philanthropy was supposed to be selfless."

"The dictionary definition of philanthropy is different in Clifton."

His eyes crinkled in the corners.

Nora explained each role in detail, and people raised their hands so she could get a head count. Then at the end of the meeting, everyone was to sign up at the front of the room. Because of the sheer number of townies, only some people who signed up would be picked for the committee, which was why it was considered an honor.

"We're not signing up, right?" Weston asked.

I shook my head. "Heck, no."

As the meeting progressed, my anxiety eased. Everyone was too focused on the committee roles versus what the actual fundraiser was in honor of—my parents, so they were barely the topic of conversation.

Nora announced it was time to sign up, and everyone formed lines at the tables. "I'm going to use the restroom really quick."

"I'll be here." Weston tucked himself in the corner of the large room by the exit.

For Wes's sake, I moved with haste, but while washing my hands, I caught myself staring into the mirror, unable to recognize the older woman in the reflection. My eyes welled when I pictured my mother and I in this exact spot, her hoisting me under my arms to reach the sink.

I never thought I would be back here.

With my head down, I left the bathroom, hoping my eyes didn't look wet. My feet skidded to a halt halfway out of the door. "Oh, I'm sorry—"

"Ivey, I'm so happy to have run into you!" Nora Lincoln stood in front of me, her cool blue eyes analyzed me, and there wasn't a short black hair out of place on her head. Her hand found its way to my upper arm, holding me gently. "How are you, sweetheart? It's been almost a decade. You look so mature now. How are you holding up?"

Her words were kind, yet her undertone felt inquisitorial.

"Hi, Nora. I've been good. How have you been?"

Her hand made lilting motions up and down my arm. "I've been great. I'm happy to see you back in town, involved in the community."

A fake smile reached my mouth before I stopped it.

She slipped her arm around my shoulder, still rubbing my back. Suddenly, I was a child again, not twenty-seven, unable to speak up for myself. Nevertheless, the urge to win her over was overwhelming. I did the thoughts from my head faster than they came, reminding myself I was not a child and my life was no longer here.

We stood in the front, far left corner of the room where we could see everyone except nobody paid attention to us.

"I heard you were planning to sell the manor."

"I never said that." I neither confirmed nor denied her comment.

Her eyes crinkled and the corners of her mouth curled. Not only could she see right through me, but I could also tell she was thinking of something to say. "I'm glad to hear that. With you back here, it's as if your parent's legacy lives on."

It felt like all my nerve impulses were stopped by her words. I was more than my parent's legacy. I was my own person, and I had my own legacy to follow. Of course, the people here didn't know anything about me or my work, and they only associated me with the success of my parents.

A success I would likely never amount to.

Nora continued, "I was thinking since this fundraiser is dedicated in their name, you could speak at the event?"

Like metal to a magnet, Weston and I locked eyes.

Even across the room, I noted the concern on his face as he watched Nora and me. He bowed his head toward the exit, wordlessly telling me it was time to get out of there.

"It's a touchy subject," I said.

She closed her eyes and nodded vigorously as if she understood.

"Just think about it, alright? You can give me a call or stop by the office, and we can devise a plan. I want you just as involved in this as me, Ivey. This fundraiser is about your family, and you deserve a say."

Well, I didn't deserve a say when you chose to exploit my parents without my consent.

"Thank you."

Before I slipped from her grasp, she placed both hands on my shoulders and leaned into my ear. "You should be careful with him."

"What?"

It took me a moment to realize we were both looking at Weston and talking about him.

"Just a motherly instinct," her words were nonchalant. "I felt it was my duty to share them since nobody else was here to tell you."

A single, blunt cackle escaped. You've got to be kidding me. I said goodbye and hurried toward the exit, unable to fathom what she had said.

Weston straightened his spine as I approached, his expression still etched with care. Neither of us spoke, though, and he didn't ask me what Nora said. Alternatively, he pressed his hand to the middle of my back and guided us out of the building.

I shoved the swell my heart made from his touch into the pits of my stomach.

"Holy shit," I exhaled, sinking into the seat. "I think I need that drink."

"Where's the closest bar?"

"Two buildings over. We could walk."

"No, we're getting out of Clifton for a little bit." He typed something into his phone and then put his car in drive. In next to no time, we were driving over the bridge. The bay—which looked like an endless black hole—encompassed us on either side as we proceeded off the island alone.

□□□□□□□□✿□□□□□□□□

I'm so sorry to leave this on a cliffhanger, I had to split this chapter into two, or else it would've been well over 5k words. I'm so excited to share chapter 11, it's one of my favorites :)

QOTD: Let's start a question chain, reply to the person below you and then post your own comment/question for people to answer!

vote • comment • follow

Thanks for reading ♡

□□□□□□□□✿□□□□□□□□

Chapter 11

Eleven | Two Beds

I T TOOK THIRTY MINUTES to pull into the waterfront bar and grill. Cars filled the lot as music and conversations with friends poured through the tavern's walls and grew louder when we pushed through the doors.

"Bar or table?"

"Bar," I told him.

The seats were congested with people of all shapes and sizes. We found two empty stools at the end of the bar so close that we had to face one other with our knees intertwining to fit. I glanced at where our skin touched, the air seeming thicker than usual.

"What do you want?"

"A gin and tonic with extra lime, please."

"Not extra gin?"

I snorted. "Unless you want to scrape me off the floor tonight."

The bartender took our orders and Weston's credit card.

"I'll pay for the next round," I said.

He shook his head, sipping his drink without breaking eye contact. I rolled my eyes.

Stevie Nicks sang Gypsy into the rustic establishment, and the smell of sweet liquor, aged wood, and the sea filled my head, making me woozy. The finish on each chair was light brown from wear and tear, and the string lights wrapped around the wooden ceiling beams glowed a pale yellow.

"Sorry I made us go tonight," I said, stirring my drink with a flimsy straw.

"Why are you apologizing? You don't have to apologize."

I didn't know why I apologized, so I dropped the subject. I thought about what Nora said before I left and asked, "How'd you find the job opening for Clifton? What made you come here?"

He stared at me, his fingers drumming on his thigh. If he moved his hand to his left, it would be touching my leg. What would his hands feel like on my skin?

"What did Nora tell you?"

My dirty thoughts melted from my brain, and my body stiffened at the mention of Nora. Should I tell him how she warned me about him? I wondered. Would that put him in a bad mood?

"She didn't tell me anything, actually. Why?"

"Nora Lincoln doesn't like me."

"I could've guessed that."

He paused and dumped his drink into his mouth until the ice clanked against the empty glass.

"I worked five, almost six years, in the intensive care unit before I became a family nurse practitioner. But I found this job through a friend in my nursing program back in New York, and I decided to take it because Clifton needed a medical professional, and I needed a job."

"Wow, I can imagine you were—are a great nurse," I corrected myself.

He chuckled curtly. His head hung like the compliment made all of the muscles in his neck snap. The sound lit up my nerve endings like a firework.

"Do you miss the ICU?"

He shrugged. "Yes and no. I miss how it challenged my brain to think and my routine, but the ICU burned me out so badly, I lost so many patients, and by year six, I was ready for no death. I wasn't taking the best care of myself, too, so to make matters even worse, I enrolled in an APRN program and worked while getting my practitioner licenses."

My skin prickled with excitement hearing about Weston's life, even if it was about work. I wanted him to keep going, so I continued. "I'm glad you're taking care of yourself now. Have you always been from New York?"

"Yeah, city boy. Born and raised." He pointed to himself, and I smiled.

"You don't really have a thick New York accent, and you don't act like a city boy."

"I don't know what that means."

"You aren't outwardly... assertive."

"Oh, I can be assertive, Sunshine." He leaned closer, and his knee slid further between my legs, closer to my core. My stomach clenched, and I fought the urge to lean back for space. "You just haven't seen it."

His proximity was short-lived, though my feelings remained.

He pulled away and ordered two more drinks.

The bartender placed two brimming glasses in front of us. I brought my still-half-full drink to my lips to chug, but Weston grabbed my wrist before I could gulp it down.

"Don't chug. We're in no rush. This one will be here when you finish."

I paused, taking in the sweet pressure of his touch. It wasn't too tight, and his thumb moved gently over my skin, sending my brain into a frenzy. His eyes were willful, despite my taught brows, and I was too distracted from how he looked at me to realize that his hand was still holding mine.

When I finally understood what he was doing, my face broke into a massive grin. "Oh, I see."

He grinned too, and I took a mental picture of how beautiful his curved mouth looked.

"I still don't understand how this correlates to Nora."

"The person who told me about the job opening was Zoe Lincoln."

Zoe? Zoe was his friend from college? A strange feeling simmered through me.

"You and Zoe went to college together?"

"Yeah, we had the same friend group. Then we both completed the same Nurse Practitioner program, but Zoe stayed in New York instead of taking over Doctor Wagner's practice. She specialized in Women's health, and the town already has an OB-GYN."

I didn't know how to react.

Zoe and Weston had slept together. Zoe had known Weston for years before us, and still, I felt protective over him, like it was just us inside this Clifton bubble, but it took three seconds for ours to pop.

"You and Zoe then?"

He finally looked at me, shaking his head. "It wasn't like that."

I had no business questioning what he did in the bedroom or who he did it with. Zoe was a lovely woman, beautiful for that matter, so I bit my tongue, downed the rest of my drink, and started working on the new one.

"It was a mistake," he added amidst our silence. "Zoe and me."

I put my hand up. "You don't have to explain it to me, Wes. You two are both consenting adults and what you do is private. I'm only sorry word got around to the entire population of Clifton."

"Yeah. People seem to think I slept my way into this position."

I stopped my jaw from hitting the table. "Seriously?"

He leaned closer. I could smell the gin on this breath. "I think Nora started that rumor because she is upset Zoe didn't take the position."

"That's quite a good guess."

I finished my second drink without him questioning me, and we ordered a third round—Rum and Cokes. I already felt the effects of the alcohol, thanks to the terribly small dinner I had eaten hours ago.

I felt my feelings clawing at my throat, wanting to come out. "You know," I rested my elbow on the counter and leaned into my hand. "I came so far after my parent's death, but ever since coming back here, it feels like I've unraveled two years of hard work," I sighed. "Nothing ever happens in Clifton, so everyone lives in this endless loop of old memories, reliving them until something new takes its place."

"Why don't you leave then?"

His question hung in the air. Why don't I leave?

"I-I'm not sure."

"I wouldn't mind fixing up the house for you."

Laughter ebbed from me, and my gaze fell to our intertwined knees. My face was scarlet and hot from the alcohol, but his offer made it even redder.

If someone had offered to fix the house before I decided to come back in the first place, I would have jumped on the opportunity. Yet, for some reason, leaving did not feel like an option.

"And leave you here alone? I don't think so."

"I've been alone for a while now. I think I'll survive."

My chest ached like someone plowed a knife inside and twisted the handle for good measure. My expression must have matched how I felt internally because he suddenly looked concerned.

"Are you feeling okay?"

"I'm just a little warm."

"Here." He held his damp, cool glass to my scorching skin. Our thighs were firmly intertwined again, and I sank into his touch. Condensation trickled down my neck and between my breasts.

We held each other gaze.

I took in every perfect line and crease of his skin. Even though we were in a room full of people, it was the first time I felt a semblance of privacy since arriving here. The longer he drank me in without speaking, the woozier I became. Do not self-sabotaging, Ivey. Do not.

My lips parted slightly when he rotated his glass and held it to the other side of my face. The tips of his fingers brushed against my cheek, and it took every muscle fiber to hold myself up.

Alcohol and I did not blend well, and the way he was earnestly looking at me was stirring up even more trouble.

"I'm going to use the restroom."

The second my feet hit the floor, all the liquor shifted in my body, plunging into the crevasses in my brain, reminding me I was not sober. But my feet did their job and carried me to a bathroom.

I locked myself in a stall and navigated my phone contacts.

"Hey, Ives," Kate's voice comforted me.

"Kate, oh, thank God. I am in a bar bathroom."

"You're in a bar bathroom? Why am I slightly jealous?" After a moment, she added. "Wait, who are you with?"

"Weston."

She paused. "Neighbor nurse?"

"Neighbor nurse." I made a strained sound. "I think it's the liquor, but he has been looking at me, Kate. Not just because he has eyes that work," I clarified and could hear her humor on the other end. "He's been looking at me in a way that makes me want to break our promise."

Her cackle almost broke my eardrum. "Ivey, I'm all for you having fun, and I'd rather get one hundred of these phone calls of you in a bar bathroom than calls of you feeling sad."

"You're not supposed to encourage me!"

"If I don't encourage you, what the hell are best friends for? I'm hanging up now." She told me she loved me before the line died, and I refrained from hitting my head off the dirty stall door, covered in graffiti.

You should be careful with him, Nora's voice echoed in my mind while leaving the bathroom to rejoin him.

When I spotted him from across the bar, I stopped to watch. He was ordering something, his body lax and his hair the slightest big a mess from him running his fingers through it. I barely knew this man, yet I felt so comfortable with him.

"You alright? I ordered water," he said, pushing a glass my way.

"I'm feeling okay, thanks." I caught the bartender's attention. "I'll take a Pineapple Upside Down, too, please."

Weston nearly choked on his water. "Oh, we're doing shots tonight?"

"I am doing a shot."

"That means I am too."

He asked the bartender to make it two as I slid back into the seat beside him.

AN HOUR LATER, Weston and I were doubled over in laughter talking about the time Kate and I made lasagna in our college apartment and dropped it inside the oven, only to scoop it out with a ladle and not eat dinner that night.

We moved to a booth in the corner where Weston wrestled my college years out of me. Now he knows all about my best friend and some of the most humiliating moments of my life.

"We put ourselves in awful situations in college. Makes me terrified to have children knowing the shit we got away with."

"I think the bottom shelf liquor we mixed altered my brain chemistry."

I wiped my watery eyes and held my sore abdomen.

Slowly I took in the room growing desolate. "Wes, how are we getting back to Clifton?"

"Walking."

"Real funny."

The drunk sheen in his eyes gleamed under the warm lights.

"We could get an Uber and pick up your car tomorrow."

He glanced at his watch; it was a quarter till twelve. "We could stay at a hotel two blocks down for the night and drive back tomorrow."

His suggestion ignited something repressed in me and my nerve endings—which must've gone senseless from the alcohol—woke up. Now I couldn't stop my forehead from burning or my muscles from tightening at the thought of staying the night with Weston.

The levelheaded part of me wanted to refuse because a hotel was a waste of money, but my reawakened spontaneity screamed one word: go.

"Okay, but let me pay since you paid for our drinks."

"Yeah, alright," he snickered, leaving the table to pay our tab. I had a feeling he was being sarcastic and was not going to let me pay for the hotel.

We left side by side, and I crossed my arms to keep myself warm against the breeze. With every wobble in my step, our shoulders brushed past one another, though I needed the friction so I would not fall over.

My fingers involuntarily traced my lips which curled up.

"Why are you laughing?"

"I am so drunk. I can't feel my lips." I tossed my head back and looked up at the night sky. "I haven't felt like this in a long time."

Walking with my eyes shut felt like I was gliding across the pavement. I stumbled, almost falling over but was yanked toward Weston's body in one firm tug. "Woah, let's keep our eyes open, maybe."

We locked gazes, his arm still secure around my shoulders. I could smell him. The sweet scent of his cologne and the salty sea emanated into my nose like almonds roasting in the mall at Christmas time. I wanted to lean closer, and nestle my cold nose into the crook of his neck, but I didn't. That was the alcohol talking.

"Thanks for taking me out tonight," I said.

Only the right side of his mouth tipped into a smile. "Any time."

His eyes scanned my face and lingered on my lips. Mine pulsed with an ache of wanting to be kissed. "My eyelids feel like paperweights, and my legs feel like led." I ran my fingers over my face, still using his body as a cane.

"Let's get you to the hotel."

We checked in around midnight. The place was more of a motel than a hotel, and it smelled the slightest bit like vinegar. The front desk receptionist chomped on her gum, peering at us over her glasses which slid down her nose. I was surprised she was still awake, but she gave us a key to room twenty-six, and Wes and I hobbled down the hallway like sneaky high-school students after prom.

"Are you okay with sleeping in the same room?"

"Oh, I don't mind," I said and the thought of us in one bed flickered in my mind. Did Wes get a room with one or two beds?

"It feels like Norman Bates is going to jump out with a knife. Ee-rr, ee-rr." I made a stabbing motion against his hard chest.

"Sorry, the reviews looked better online."

I stopped walking altogether and said, "Don't apologize."

Humor laced his face. "Okay."

He inserted the key, and the room was surprisingly cleaner than I anticipated. Unlike the reception desk area, this room smelled Pine-Sol and looked straight out of a nineties ad catalog. The walls were green and there were two beds with matching ornate red duvets.

Two beds.

I ignored the flicker of disappointment that coursed through me.

"Can you stand for a second?" He leaned me against the wall like I was a broom, then began stripping the duvet from the bed closest to the window and inspected each corner of the mattress.

"What the hell are you doing?"

"Checking for bed bugs."

I scrunched my nose up. "That's disgusting."

"I don't see any sign of them." He pulled the flat sheet down and waved me over. "Alright, you can sit now."

I wobbled toward him and fell flat onto the mattress. My body bounced once, and I laughed, even though my head was spinning. It took me a moment to realize I was in a motel, alone with Weston, incredibly drunk.

"Let me."

I felt his hands lift my foot from the mattress as he slid my shoes off one by one. I wiggled my toes from the freedom, and propped myself up on my elbows, watching him.

He seemed more clearheaded than I was, or maybe he handled his liquor better.

"I'm like one of your patients."

It was his turn to look disgusted. "Don't say that."

"You haven't scheduled a check-up to see my foot." I held up the affected limb, which healed quite nicely after tending to it for two weeks. He held my ankle, stood between my legs at the edge of the bed, and looked down at me.

This was quite a compromising position.

"You're supposed to schedule the follow-up with my secretary."

"Hmm," I pretended to think, matching his playfulness. "I want my follow-up now."

Narrowing his eyes, he inspected my foot, tilting it in all different directions like it would help him see better. "Looks like it's healing beautifully." He gently set it on the mattress and began stripping the other bed. His bed.

I hobbled to the bathroom, washing my face and cleaning my mouth as best as possible without my toothbrush. Though the joy of being drunk was I didn't care about how I looked or that I was not showering before bed, I wanted to curl up in the foreign room and fall asleep.

I used the towel to blot my face dry, then Weston and I switched places.

He closed the bathroom door, the bright light seeped through the cracks and I heard the shower turn on. I groaned.

Did he and Zoe spend drunken nights like this in college?

Stop it, Ivey.

Unable to sleep in anything, my folded jeans and bra tucked underneath found a home on the nightstand. I kept my sweater on for Weston's sake and slid under the covers, which had the faintest aroma of an indoor pool.

The room was sticky with steam when Weston reentered the bedroom. I made a mental note to glance at him, except the state between asleep and awake consumed me and my eyes would not budge open.

The edge of my bed dipped. Wes's fingers grazed my shoulders as he tugged the blanket up my body and whispered goodnight before I fell into a deep slumber.

□□□□□□□□❀□□□□□□□□

Happy December, friends ♥

QOTD: Favorite song in rotation right now?

vote • comment • follow

Thanks for reading ♡

❑❑❑❑❑❑❑❑✿❑❑❑❑❑❑❑

Chapter 12
Twelve | Take Out

T w: parental death, loss/death

WESTON DROPPED ME OFF at my front door the following day with a honk and waved goodbye. He drove home to Masie, who was likely wondering where her owner had been all night. With trashed Ivey.

Not turning on a single light, I stripped while walking through my bedroom and bathroom. With my robe and towel in hand, I made buttered toast and poured a glass of ice water, then stood at the foot of the stairs leading up to my parent's bedroom.

Unless I was gathering fresh linens or cleaning supplies, I had not been upstairs in any bedrooms since I got back. There was no need. Yet, my parent's clawfoot tub, which overlooked the bay, called my name.

After a long exhale, I hiked upstairs and pushed into my parent's room through the double doors. Their scent caged me, and I had to grip the door frame.

The floor-to-ceiling Chinoiserie curtains were taught, though the tiniest streak of light beamed across the room like a speckled wall of gold. Their sheets were slick and adorned with blue throw pillows.

The room appeared frozen in time.

My mom's perfume bottles and jewelry littered the dresser, and my father's ties hung over the wicker rocking chair beside the bay window. The same window seat I occasionally sleep on and watch the beams from the lighthouse revolve in a steady rhythm.

My shoulders sagged. "Hi, mom and dad."

The tile was cold on my toes as I opened the window shades and drew a bath. With effort, I avoided looking in the mirror because I knew I looked as bad as I felt, and I was surprised I survived thirty minutes in the car without puking.

My phone hummed with a text from Weston. Make sure you eat and drink water today. Don't skip meals.

My cheeks dimpled, and I glanced at his house, which I had a perfect view of from this window. I have buttered toast and water. Super nutritious. Getting into the bath to soak away the scent of the motel.

Except the buttered toast was not sitting well in my stomach, and just before I stepped into the tub, my cheeks began to water, and I bolted to the toilet, puking up all of the content inside of my stomach.

So much for trying to be proactive.

Leaning against the cool wall, I texted back, Never mind. Buttered toast came back up.

He sent back a frowning face. Come by the office. I'll give you IV fluids.

Even though he was joking, I chuckled, holding my stomach. The last thing I would want to do was go to work and the fact that he had to go into the office today made me doubly queasy; for him and me. I had never been more thankful for my computer.

My muscles felt like jello as I lowered myself into the tub and cracked the window. The hot water engulfed my body while my head was chilly from the bracing scent of damp earth blowing into the room.

I watched the bay water lap against Weston's dock, and my fingers involuntarily grazed my shoulder where his fingers touched last night.

Wes was nothing like I imagined he would be. He was kind and gentle, and that stupid, beautiful smile I had waited so long to see was engrained in my brain as though it was branded with a hot iron.

Above all, it felt good to sit and laugh with someone.

When I randomly woke in the middle of the night, still drunk and startled that I was not in my own bed. I focused on the sound of Weston's soft breathing. My eyes squinted to get a better look, and I turned on my side.

Even though his face was only slightly visible, the faint light from the bathroom (which we left on, so neither of us tripped in the middle of the night) highlighted his lips squished against the pillow. He was lying on his stomach with his arms above his head, underneath his pillow. The sheet covered most of his body, but his biceps were bare. I swallowed, knowing his torso was too.

He looked so handsome and peaceful that I watched the rise and fall of his shoulders until sleep consumed me again.

After my bath, I threw up one more time and called to tell Kate about last night. Unable to stand the light, I got into old Christmas pajamas, curled up in my dark bedroom, and slept the day away even though I needed to get work done.

Never again will I have that many Pineapple Upside Downs in such a short period, but if I could transport back to last night with Weston, I would.

HOT AIR WARMED my hand, and after one wet lick, my eyes sprang open to find Masie panting at the side of my bed. She sat perfectly upright, her tail wagging back and forth and her tongue hanging lopsided.

My entire face scrunched. "Masie? How did you get in here?"

That's when I heard Weston demandingly calling Masie's name in a whisper. My heart sprang to life, and so did the rest of my body. The dog didn't budge for her owner, and she waited for me to reach out and stroke her head—which I did.

"Ivey?" He murmured my name.

Oh gosh, he was coming closer. I pretended I was out cold.

Weston's footsteps rounded the corner and stopped at my bedroom door. "Masie, come here. Now." His voice was stern but quiet, and I knew she listened from the jingling of her collar.

My room was atrocious, with clothes strewn on every piece of furniture. If my mom saw the state of this room—which I was never allowed in when I was younger since it was a guest room—I would have been scolded.

The corner of the bed dipped. "Ivey? Hey, it's almost five."

I blinked. Was it that late? I had slept that long? "Wes?"

"Hi, sorry to barge in." He rubbed the back of his neck. "You weren't answering any of my calls. I knocked on the door for a while, and you weren't answering either. I opened it to make sure you didn't suffocate on your vomit or anything, and Masie ran in."

"I appreciate the concern. I'm okay, just incredibly hung over."

He laughed. "I figured. Have you eaten?"

"Not since throwing up that single piece of toast."

His eyes narrowed in reprimand. "Well, I brought takeout."

I sat up a little too fast. "You did not have to do that."

"What if I said I bought too much for myself and need someone to share it with?"

"Much better. You can pick a place to eat. I'm gonna change." I needed him out of my room, not only because I needed to brush my teeth but because I didn't want to show my reaction to him coming over to check on me and bring food. "Feel free to dig in the kitchen cabinets if you need anything."

He left the room, giving me space to toss dirty clothes into the hamper, slip on a crewneck and yoga pants, and fix myself in the bathroom. My face still looked like someone had taken a frying pan to each eye, but there was nothing I could do about that.

I joined him on the back patio. Open food containers were strewn across the coffee table, and he knelt on the ground. "There is Chicken Tikka Masala, Chicken Curry, Rice, and garlic Naan."

I nearly groaned, but my stomach did before my mouth could. It smelled heavenly. "I can't say thank you enough. What do I owe?"

He ignored me like last night, and I nudged his arm. "Hey, don't ignore me. You paid for drinks, the motel, and this." He kept eating. "Tell. Me. What. I. Owe." My fist punched his biceps between each word.

A smile seeped through his stoic expression, and he nearly lost his grip on his food from my blows. "Okay, okay, alright! This was my payment for you watching and bathing Masie. Accept it and move on."

"Fine, but I am paying next time."

I held my hand out to make a pact, and he hesitated before conjoining and firmly shaking. I let the delicious strength of touch bleed into my palm, and we shook until our hands fell still, then apart.

"Are you feeling any better?"

"Yeah, now that I wasted the entire day. I haven't been drunk like that in a while. My body had a hard time adjusting." I took a bite of food; the creamy sweet, and spicy chicken melted in my mouth, and I closed my eyes in pure bliss. "How about you?"

"I felt terrible, too, but I had appointments I couldn't miss."

"Sorry, I'm a terrible influence."

"I don't mind. I had a great time."

We looked at each other, our eyes addressing everything that occurred without talking about it.

"Oregon state. What made you go the whole way there?" He pointed to my shirt.

"Oh, yeah." I glanced down as if I had forgotten what my favorite sweatshirt looked like. "I lived on the East coast my entire life and wanted to see what the West coast was all about. Plus, I wanted to get as far away as possible."

"And how was it?"

"I loved it. It's so different compared to here." I listed all the notable differences between the coasts and explained how I had been fortunate enough to travel all over the states for my graduate degree and job.

"I bet your parents were proud."

"Yeah, they were."

Silence consumed us.

"How have you been doing?"

I knew he was asking about my parents.

"I've been better." I laughed.

"I imagine all of the fundraiser stuff has drudged a lot of feelings up."

My back rested against the couch I wasn't sitting on. Instead, I sat crisscrossed on the floor across from Weston. I assumed he had looked up what happened to my parents already, or someone had told him whatever story they were fed. For the first time, it bothered me to think that he knew a story from a completely different source.

"Weston, do you know what happened to my parents?"

He hesitated; those brown eyes studied me. "I know they were out doing research and that it was tragic."

"Are you comfortable hearing the whole story?"

"Are you comfortable telling me?" he countered.

A lump formed in my throat from those five words.

I gnawed on the inside of my cheek, hoping the pain would overpower the ache from swallowing. Nobody ever asked if I was comfortable talking about their deaths, and most wanted to hear the morbid details. And deep down, I'm sure Weston was just as interested as everyone else, but the fact that he cared more about my comfort than his curiosity spoke volumes.

"Yes, I'm comfortable. I would rather you hear from me than from a random news outlet or stranger in town."

He stood up, holding his hand out. "Let's go sit outside."

I took his hand, neglecting to put shoes on. He guided me down my dock, and Masie trailed behind. My eyes shut, and I counted my steps even though Weston was beside me. If he saw me, he didn't ask what I was doing.

We sat opposite of one another, our backs against a pillar. Masie curled up beside me. Could she sense my anxiousness?

"I'm all ears," he said.

"Well, it was a little over two years ago; going to be three soon." I let out a shaky breath, listening to the lapping water. "My parents were self-employed and published their own research journals for most of their life. They refused most traditional deals because they wanted control of their profits. They gave chunks of their earnings to environmental or wildlife organizations while still keeping enough to live comfortably. After they built a name for themselves, they started taking on other projects for companies, like cameos in magazines or assistance with research projects.

I paused. "Sometimes I wonder if I was an accident, you know? Why did they decide to have a child if they traveled a lot during my childhood? But looking back on everything they did, they were so driven, and they gave me this life," I motioned to the house and land around me. "I'm incredibly thankful for it."

He nodded.

"Anyway, I was in my apartment in Seattle with Kate when it happened. I remember it being so stormy that year. There were hurricane warnings for most coastal states, especially here in Maryland. One thing about being self-employed was they did everything, I mean everything, themselves. They didn't go out with huge research teams or have all the equipment necessary to stay safe when they were out in the wild. They had enough to get by and, most importantly, their satellite phone."

Memories came flooding back of Kate and me rushing around our apartment, and I fought back the tears. "They called me two days before they went on that trip and didn't tell me what project it was. We had our routine anytime they went researching: call in the morning and a call at night to let me know they were safe. They called me for two days, and then there were no calls on the third day. The news reported terrible storms off the coast with flooding and rough waters."

I stared into the grey water. "They wouldn't pick up their phone, and I had this terrible empty feeling. I didn't know what to do, so I called the police and the coastguard. It took five days, but they were found on some island they weren't supposed to be on. All their stuff was gone, washed out to sea, including the boat they took. They were found together, suspected to have died from dehydration and hypothermia."

Weston stared, not speaking.

Something wet dribbled down my neck, and I reached up to find my face soaked with tears. The realization I was crying caused me to gulp air, and my lungs burned as they stretched from holding my breath.

"I didn't have a funeral, but I had them buried in the Clifton cemetery. People found out and were furious. They called me apathetic and selfish for not having a public funeral to let them grieve or celebrate their lives. To be honest, the rest is kind of a blur. I don't remember locking up the house and leaving, but this is the first time I have been back since."

That was the first time I had told the entire story since therapy. Usually, I gave the abridged version, or people already knew what happened, and I didn't care to give details.

I waited for Weston to say something, but he just watched me. His expression was not pitiful but caring. After a moment, he finally spoke.

"My first year in the ICU, I cared for a twenty-four-year-old patient who wasn't much older than me. He came to the ER after getting in a motorcycle accident, then to my unit. I took care of him for weeks, trying to keep him stable. He recovered. He was smiling, cracking jokes, walking occasionally." Weston smiled too.

"He was changing to a med-surge floor since he was no longer an ICU patient. Then one shift, he grabbed my arm and told me something felt really wrong, and I told him it would be okay. Minutes later, I was doing CPR, but it wasn't enough. We lost him, and I still see his face to this day. He died after I told him it would be okay."

He picked at the skin on his fingers. "So, Ivey, the point of the story is I am not going to tell you it will be okay because who knows if it will. Emotions aren't linear, and they don't follow a perfect curve. They're messy, they come and go, but the nice thing is that sometimes we get to decide how much effort we put into recognizing when we may need more support or when we just need to feel sad."

I covered my face and released an exasperated laugh which turned into a stomach-clenching cackle. It was terrible timing, but I couldn't stop. My hands cupped my face as my laughter morphed into sobs.

My emotions felt like someone spilled water on a live wire. I was relieved to cry, embarrassed that it was in front of Wes, yet thankful for the conversation. "I'm sorry I'm crying."

I felt the dock shift before arms encompassed me. "You're allowed to cry."

Weston sat on my right and pulled my body into his warm grasp. Instinctively, I rested my arm on his shoulder, and at that moment,

I had never been so thankful for having him here or having a friend (other than Kate) who genuinely cared.

"Thank you for sharing the story about your patient. I'm sure it wasn't easy."

"Thank's for telling me about your parents."

"Do you believe in ghosts?" I asked.

"I'm not sure. Do you?"

I nodded. "I feel like my parents are here in this house."

"I'm sure they are with you."

"I also think Mr. Morris's ghost is with you in your house," I said, and now he was laughing.

"I haven't seen him, but if I do, I'll let him know you're thinking about him too."

The humor between us dwindled, and my heartbeat slowed. We sat like that for a while, watching the gray water turning darker as the sun slowly lost its shine. It felt normal sitting here with him, my head resting on his shoulder.

"Thanks again," I whispered.

"Anytime."

Chapter 13

Thirteen | The Marshlands

T HE WEEKEND PASSED and the remnants of my hangover were gone but the conversations Weston and I had were fresh in my mind. It felt good to tell him about my parents instead of wondering what he already knew.

I was thankful for his story about the hospital. Death was brutal, no matter how close you were to the passing person, and Weston reminded me I was not alone in grief.

I tucked my backpack—which housed my parent's research and camera—inside the boat and started the engine. Weston's house was dark, and his car was missing, yet I saw Masie's face in the window and waved as if she knew I was saying hello.

Since I fell behind on the project Larry assigned, I spent the morning completing a large chunk of the paper and forwarding it to the magazine team. I had time to myself before dinner and was eager to take more pictures for my parent's journal.

The discontent over their secret Clifton research slowly morphed into excitement I forgot was possible to feel, especially toward work. Even if nothing were to come of the journal, working on it made me feel a part of their legacy, and it made me feel closer to them.

The current yanked and pulled at the boat. My grip on the wheel tightened as I slid through rougher waves toward the Marshlands. When the bow thudded against the mud, my shoulders slumped in relief, and I wiped the saltwater from my face.

I spent the next hour taking photos and notes on different plants and specimens. The sky slowly shifted from a misty blue to a dull grey. I checked the radar. A storm was brewing, even though it was not supposed to earlier, and I was on land likely to flood with the downpour.

I hustled around for ten minutes, gathering as much information as possible, and hopped back in my boat. The engine roared over the crashing waves, the mainland grew closer, and the Lincoln residence came into view.

It looked even more grandeur now than it did in my memory.

A figure crouched by the shore, holding a basket. From the short dark hair blowing beneath the floppy hat (which protected her from nothing and was instead there for aesthetic), I knew it was Nora herself. I hadn't seen her since the last meeting, before I learned about Zoe's history with Weston and before she warned me about her motherly instinct.

She stood, waving me in her direction. I could see her lips moving but could not make out what she was saying, so I slowed, and my boat drifted toward their dock from the current.

"Ivey is that you? I can spot your parent's boat a mile away!" she shouted.

"Hello, Nora."

She clasped a hand to her heart. "It's going to storm, Hun'. Do you wanna come inside before it hits? You can park in our boat garage."

"Thank you for the offer, but I should head back."

"Nonsense, come and have tea!"

Like a child being told what to do, I drove toward their boat garage. The door rolled open and I pulled in to meet Nora.

"Excuse my attire. I was gardening." She waved me off, but her white and blue striped button-up, sleek pants, and rain boots looked perfect compared to my dirty overalls. Although, I did not expect her to do yard work.

I left my backpack in the storage container under the seat and followed Nora into her house. The slim memories I had of this house came rushing back as we walked toward the cream and grey colored stone and wood exterior.

While my childhood home was ornate with deep red shades and rustic brown furniture, the inside of Nora's home was cool in color and temperature and smelled like lemons, and it looked more like a show house than a lived-in space.

Nora neatly took her boots off by the back door. So, I did too.

"Take a seat wherever you'd like. Is Earl Grey fine?"

I told her yes and brushed the lingering dirt from my pants before sitting on the light blue cushions.

"Not the best day for boating, hmm?" she said, filling a teapot with the pasta arm.

"I guess not." I glanced at the sparse raindrops hitting the window. "Not a good day for gardening either."

"Unfortunately not. What were you doing out in the marsh?"

It was an innocent question, but it felt prying. "Just going for a ride, observing nature."

She smiled, placing two tea bags in matching mugs. "You remind me so much of your mother, and you know she used to stop by for tea all the time."

"Did she?"

"Yes, which means you are also welcome to come over anytime. The house gets lonely with only Tom and me here." She set a steaming mug on the table and sat opposite me. "I know Zoe has been away for years, but I'm still not used to having an empty nest."

Zoe's name triggered the image of Weston. "How's Zoe doing? Where'd she end up living?" I asked, even though I knew. A strange expression tugged on Nora's face.

"Zoe is working as a Women's Health Nurse Practitioner in New York."

I acted surprised and avoided mentioning another Nurse Practitioner I knew we both were thinking of. Before I could say anything else, Nora continued. "It's a shame you were in different graduating classes. I feel like you both would have been best friends. She's coming to visit soon; you should plan to go for coffee."

My skin prickled, and I sat straighter. "Zoe's coming to visit?"

"Yes, she's coming home to visit and helping with the fundraiser."

Nora kept talking, but I interacted on autopilot, my brain filled with thoughts of Zoe and Weston seeing each other again.

I felt guilty for my territorial feelings over Wes, but he was my only true friend right now and the only person I felt safe with sharing my feelings.

Did he know she was coming back?

He told me there was nothing between him and Zoe. Of course, I believed him, but she was a direct tether to Nora, who currently was someone I did not fully trust, considering she had tight control over what the public should and shouldn't know. I know she was one of the main reasons people had poor opinions about me, the estranged daughter.

"I was doing some thinking, and we need to involve you more in planning this event. It will be healing for you to be a part of the committee and have people around you who care.

Emotions clawed at my throat, a mixture of sadness and irritation. I pushed the handle of my mug back and forth to distract myself. "Thanks, Nora. I'll think about it."

She reached across the table and cupped my hands. Her skin was incredibly soft, certainly not a pair of hands that gardened, but the contact made my heart swell. It was a mother's touch, a forgotten feeling.

Before I left, she wrote down her phone number, and somehow, I made it out without shedding a tear. Even when I got into my boat, against her request to stay until the drizzling stopped, I did not let the tears fall because I wasn't sure what I'd be crying over.

The waves were rougher than usual, but I kept a stern grip on the wheel as I sailed through the inlet. As I turned the corner, Weston's house lights glistened on the rippling water, a beacon of warmth through the dark afternoon. I smiled.

On cue, his back door opened, and he walked onto his porch, cupping his hands around his mouth. "Do you have a death wish?"

I eased off the gas. "I'm just enjoying the weather!"

"Do you wanna enjoy the weather from inside my house?"

I stared blankly, wondering if I had heard him right. "Right now?"

"Yes!"

Nerves churned through me, yet I shrugged, pretending I felt passive about entering his house.

I met him at the end of his dock, where we tied my boat, then dashed down the slippery wood, the rain pelting us from behind. Masie jumped at the back door excited, and her panting fogged the window.

When he closed the door behind us, pine, cinnamon, and heat engulfed me like a hug.

The walls drowned out the sound of the rain but only amplified my beating heart. I couldn't put my feelings into words. Bittersweet? Enamored? Peculiar?

Growing up, I had the perfect view of The Blue House from my bedroom. It was in the background of my childhood memories, but I had never been inside. Though, it was nothing like I imagined.

There were no cobwebs, no broken floorboards, or peeling ancient wallpaper. Between the crackling fireplace and table lamps, the living room—centered in the heart of the house—glowed a delicate orange.

"Wow, this place is nothing like I imagined."

"Is that a good or bad thing?"

"A good thing," I chuckled. "I have never been here, even though we live across the water. I thought it was haunted for most of my life, so I was terrified."

He guided me into the white wooden kitchen with dark brown exposed ceiling beams and offered something to drink. I accepted a cup of coffee, even though it would be my third today. What was sleep for anyways?

"Oh yeah, that's what you mentioned the other night. I hear the floorboards creaking sometimes, but I chalk it up to the house settling."

"Mmhm... or maybe it is Mr. Morris trying to reclaim his property."

"Maybe. Was he mean?"

"Not at all. He definitely had some spunk in him, though," I said, then apologized as if Mr. Morris could hear. "He would always ask where my parents were when I roamed around the backyard alone, and I think he knew they left me home alone."

"How old were you?"

"I was eleven when they started leaving me home alone."

"Wow. Eleven is young."

My shoulders bounced. "I got used to it fast."

He motioned for me to follow him into the living room. He settled into the armchair beside the fireplace and told me to sit anywhere I wanted. Naturally, I curled into the corner of the felt, emerald-green couch adjacent to him.

"Did you have a good day at work?"

"It was fine. Did you work today? Is that why you were out on your boat in terrible weather?"

"I sent my boss the finalized article for our magazine this morning, then went out on the water for fun. I didn't realize it was supposed to rain, but you'll never believe who I had tea with."

"Who?"

"Nora Lincoln."

His mouth hung open loosely. "Why? How?"

I laughed at his reaction. "She saw me in my boat and asked if I wanted to come inside while it rained. For some reason, I had a hard time saying no, so we had tea and talked about the fundraiser. She said she really wants me involved since it will be very 'healing' for me." I used air quotes, his eyes wide like saucers.

"Did you tell her she should've asked permission?"

"I don't know if she knows what permission means."

I should have mentioned Zoe was coming to Clifton, but I figured he knew since the two likely talked. Instead, I told him why I was out on the water and dug my parent's journal out of my backpack.

"I found this in my parent's den." He reached over to the coffee table for the leather-bound booklet. "Every page is dated right before their passing."

He paused before flipping through the pages.

"Apparently, they were researching Clifton, which I found odd when I first found the journal. They promised never to make Clifton their job, so I've wondered why they randomly decided to start this project. After I stopped being annoyed with them for not telling me, I contemplated finishing the book on their behalf."

"What made you come to that decision?" he asked genuinely.

I took a moment to think. "I guess it's something I can do to honor them."

He scanned my face, then closed the book. "You're not having these feelings because of the fundraiser, right?"

"What do you mean?"

"You don't have to do anything physical to honor your parents, Ivey."

I adjusted my legs under my body, suddenly feeling defensive. "I know I don't."

"Alright," he said, still not breaking eye contact.

Uncomfortable silence loomed between us. The crackling logs and rain filled the homely space. I brought my mug to my lips, staring at the non-fiction books stacked in the corner of the room. I took note of the lack of pictures on the wall and mantle.

"Ivey," Weston's voice sliced through the room.

"Ives, I'm sorry if that was harsh," he said when I didn't react, but every nerve ending in my body awoke from the nickname. "I just want you to know that appreciating or honoring your parents internally is enough. Not everything has to be for a show like they do here in Clifton, and you don't owe anyone any proof of your love for them."

"Ives?" I repeated, trying to lighten the mood I almost killed again.

The lines across his forehead softened, and his eyes were full of amusement. "Really? That's all you heard out of that pep talk?"

I nodded. "Yes, Wes."

"Wes?"

"That's my nickname for you. Also, Mr. I-don't-like-to-smile."

His smile faded faster than it appeared. "What do you mean, Mr. I-don't-like-to-smile? I like to smile."

"Barely."

"I save my smile for special occasions," he clarified.

"Ahh, I understand. We must be careful showing our happiness around here, and we wouldn't want anyone stealing it away."

"Exactly."

Our laughter died down. He admired me like the night in the bar, with the same softness in his eyes and undivided attention. His gentle smile did not falter, and neither did mine, as we enjoyed each other's quiet company and contentment.

"I should probably head home." I pushed myself off the couch. "Thank's for the coffee."

He stood, taking my mug. "Yeah, of course."

"I have to run to the grocery store tomorrow after work, and I can pick up something to make for dinner. You know, to thank you for watching Masie the other day."

He did not just invite me over for dinner.

I kept my excitement at bay as I agreed to dinner and climbed into my boat for the last time today. No tears threatened to spill now, as I boated home for the night.

CPSIA information can be obtained
at www.ICGtesting.com
Printed in the USA
LVHW080549280223
740519LV00015B/260

9 781805 095569